ONe
iN A
HUNDReD
THOUSAND

With thanks to Jenny Child from the Child Growth Foundation

First published in the UK in 2021 by Usborne Publishing Ltd., Usborne House,
83-85 Saffron Hill, London EC1N 8RT, England. www.usborne.com
Usborne Verlag, Usborne Publishing Ltd., Prüfeninger Str. 20,
93049 Regensburg, Deutschland, VK Nr. 17560

Text copyright © Linn Irene Ingemundsen, 2021

A CIP catalogue record for this book is available from the British Library.

FMAMJJASOND/20 ISBN 9781474940641 04697/1

Printed and bound in Great Britain by CPI Group (UK) Ltd, Croydon, CR0 4YY

MIX
Paper from
responsible sources
FSC
www.fsc.org
FSC® C020471

ONE IN A HUNDRED THOUSAND

LINNI INGEMUNDSEN

USBORNE

I failed another test. It must have been the third one in four weeks. I didn't fail because of my condition. It didn't happen because I'm dumb.

Failing on purpose is actually not as easy as it sounds. You need to make sure you miss over fifty-five per cent of the test without making it obvious. So you can't put down any ridiculous answers or anything. If you can't think of something that sounds close, but definitely isn't right, it's better to just leave it blank or put down a question mark. Okay, it actually is pretty easy.

I'm not sure if the fact that I have been doing this on purpose makes it better or worse. There was a plan behind it. Not a very good one I suppose, but there was a plan.

Apart from my recent underachieving at school, I'm pretty much just like everyone else. At the same time I'm not. I like gaming, hanging out with my friends and reading comics. And I like taking pictures, but I don't know if I'm good at it. I only have about a hundred and fifty followers on Instagram. But maybe that just means I'm not very popular.

I have two brothers. Jakob is seventeen, two years older than me. He drives a moped and has loads of friends. And girls love him. My younger brother, Adrian, is fourteen. He is stronger than me and faster than me. And, just like everyone else on the planet, he is also taller than me.

My dad died when I was six years old. He was a fisherman. He had broad shoulders and big arms. One day he went out to sea. And he didn't come back. My brothers both look a lot like him. I don't.

I have narrow shoulders and skinny arms and a tiny waist.

My right arm is longer than my left arm.

I am fifteen years old and 153 centimetres tall. The average height for an adult male in Norway is 179.7 centimetres. I'm not anywhere near average.

I figure the school will eventually contact my mum and tell her what's going on. I haven't been in trouble before. It's not like I am a star student or anything, but I always get by. For the past few days I have expected her to say something but so far nothing has happened. Every day she just comes home from work and everything is normal.

Earlier today, around 5 p.m., I had gone into the kitchen to get a glass of water just as Mum walked in carrying a grocery bag in each hand. I tried to read her facial expression, but I couldn't tell if she looked mad or not.

"Oh, hey," she said when she noticed me. There was nothing unusual about her voice either.

I sat down at the table and watched her put away the groceries. She placed two packets of chicken fillets on the counter, which I guessed meant we'd be having them for dinner. With a hundred per cent certainty I knew the chicken would be organic, because we can't eat chicken unless it is organic. That would just be insane.

I wasn't sure if the reason Mum didn't say anything was because she hadn't heard anything from the school yet, or if she was just torturing me. I couldn't take the suspense any longer, I had to know.

So I said, "How was your day?"

She looked up and paused for a minute. "It was fine." Then she gave me a sceptical look. "Why do you ask?"

I shrugged. "Do I need a reason?"

She lowered her shoulders and smiled. "No, of course not. It was very nice of you to ask. How was your day?"

"Fine."

"Did something happen?"

"Nope." I got up from my chair. "I've got homework."

"Okay," she said. "Dinner will be ready in about an hour."

I went upstairs to my room and started on my homework. I could hear music playing from the next room, which meant that Adrian was home. Not that this was a surprise to me or anything, because most of the time he wouldn't be out somewhere without me knowing where he was. I know this is going to sound really, really lame but my younger brother is actually my best friend.

There were no sounds coming from Jakob's room, which made sense as it was Tuesday and he would be at handball practice.

For Norwegian class, I had to read a poem by Rolf Jacobsen and answer questions about it. It was something about machines eating trees and how this was some sort of hell for wise pelicans. It didn't make much sense to me.

There were five questions connected to the poem and I didn't really have to do much faking when answering them poorly.

I finished my work, and then Mum called us down for dinner. I closed my workbook and ran downstairs two steps at a time. When I reached the bottom of the stairs, I heard Adrian opening the door to his room.

In my mind, we had a race and I won. If he had been aware of the race he would have beaten me, so it was better that he didn't know.

I walked into the kitchen and took a seat at the table, opposite Mum. Adrian came in and sat down next to me. No matter if we are all home or not, we always sit in the same places.

Then we ate our organic chicken with steamed vegetables and brown rice. No one was really talking, because everyone was busy on their phones.

Shortly after, we could hear someone opening and closing the front door, which was soon followed by a loud thud. It was Jakob, dumping his gym bag on the floor. Next we could hear the sound of his shoes hitting the wall as he kicked them off. My mum hates it when he does that, but she didn't say anything as he walked into the kitchen. She just said "Hi", hardly looking up from her phone.

Jakob's cheeks were red and he smelled like the wind.

"Hey," he said and sat down next to Mum, opposite Adrian. He helped himself to the food but skipped the rice. Carbs are apparently very bad for you if you want to make it as a handball player.

Me, I eat all the carbs I can get. My mum put away her phone and asked Jakob how his practice went. For a while we talked about how many goals he had scored, and then we talked about how Adrian finally managed to do this bike trick he has been working on. No one talked about me failing my maths test, because apparently my school is really slow at picking up on these things. You would think they'd pay extra attention to someone like me.

This is what Google has to say about Silver-Russell syndrome:

Silver-Russell syndrome (SRS) is one of many growth disorders. It is characterized by a slow growth, starting even before the baby is born. Many children with SRS have low muscle tone and may start to sit up and walk later than average. Some may also have delayed speech development. Signs and symptoms may include; low birth weight, a head that appears large in relation to body size, poor appetite, characteristic facial features including a prominent forehead or a small, triangular-shaped face; and arms and legs of different lengths.

What Google doesn't tell you is what it *feels* like to be the shortest boy in your class. Or how it feels to know that this isn't going to change.

Approximately one in a hundred thousand people has Silver-Russell syndrome.

My name is Sander Dalen.

I am one in a hundred thousand.

A couple of days later I woke up before the alarm clock. I opened my desk drawer and took out a pencil. Then I stood next to the door frame. I made sure to stand up properly and look straight ahead and not go up on my tiptoes. Then I took the pencil and made a mark on the door frame above my head. I turned around to look at it. The mark was in the exact same spot as before. I sighed and got dressed, because what else can you do?

When I walked into the kitchen, Frank, the family dog, was standing by the door wagging his tail and looking at me with begging eyes. He is a Jackabee, which is a mix between a beagle and a Jack Russell terrier.

"Someone needs to take Frank for his walk," Mum said, walking into the kitchen.

The sound of the word "walk" and his name made Frank let out a little bark.

Jakob was sitting at the table, eating cereal.

"Not me," he said, without looking up from his bowl.

"I'll take him," I said.

I went into the hallway, closely followed by Frank, and put my shoes and coat on before putting the lead on him. It had been classic end-of-summer/beginning-of-autumn weather recently. Sunny one day, and cold the next. But, in the last week or so, autumn had fully set in, which meant a lot of wind and rain ahead.

I'm often the one who takes Frank for his walks. I don't mind, because it also gives me the opportunity to take pictures at the same time. I have a vintage Olympus 35 RC camera with a 42 mm lens that used to belong to my dad. I feel a bit silly taking my camera out with me in public, but if Frank's there I already have a reason to be out and I feel less awkward. I normally don't take my camera out on his morning walks, though. There's not a lot of time to take pictures before school.

If someone were to ask me if I like digital or analogue cameras better, I wouldn't know what to answer. I like digital photographs because the images are very clear, and you can easily upload them to social media and crop, adjust the light and add filters as you please. And if you mess up, you can just take a new one. But, at the same time, it makes people care less about making an effort.

They just push the button over and over until they get the result they want. What I like about analogue cameras is that you have to be more careful. You have to think about the lighting, the angle and the composition before you push the button, because you don't want to waste film. And you won't know if the pictures were successful or not until the film is developed. Waiting for the results might be my favourite part of analogue photography. It is kind of like opening a birthday present or waiting for a parcel in the post. Sometimes the anticipation is the best part.

I often take Frank to this little forest just a short walk from our house. To get there I have to pass old Kåland's house. He is the town loner. I don't know what his first name is. I am not sure he even has one.

When we were younger we used to pull pranks on him all the time. Like egging his house or ringing his doorbell and running away. Normally I wasn't a fan of games where we had to be fast and run away, because I would always fall behind, but Kaland wasn't much of a runner. He would normally stop by the end of his driveway and yell empty threats after us like, "Just you wait!" or "I'll get you!"

Sometimes we'd sneak into his backyard to steal plums from his trees. His basement windows were nailed shut so we couldn't see what was going on in there, but everyone agreed that he was doing something illegal. Like whitewashing money, running a meth lab or burying dead bodies. I doubt that these theories are true, but he is definitely mad. He is like a crazy cat lady, except he is a man. Who doesn't have cats.

Even though I was used to Kaland doing weird things, I was still taken aback when I saw his house that morning. Because this was new. He has a couple of pine trees in his front yard, and one of them was decorated like a Christmas tree. With lights and baubles and all kinds of different ornaments.

It was September.

I actually hadn't seen him for a while, and for all I knew he could have moved away. Or died. He had to be pretty old by now, I guess. He was already old when we were kids. We pretty much lost interest in him when we grew up, so I didn't know what he'd been up to. But no one else would decorate a Christmas tree in September, so I supposed that proved he was still there.

Frank had disappeared behind some trees, and as I was waiting for him to do his thing I got my phone out of my pocket and opened up the camera.

I held my phone up and took a picture of the tree. Suddenly a light came on in Kaland's house and I quickly put the phone back in my pocket. I really didn't want him to see me there, because he kind of gives me the creeps.

And even though I hadn't seen him in a long time, he probably would have known that I was one of the kids who used to egg his house. Because we are all one of the kids who used to egg his house.

I tugged Frank's lead slightly.

"Come on," I said, "hurry up."

After a few minutes, Frank's white and brown head appeared from behind the trees and he let out a little bark, running ahead.

I picked up after him and hurried home.

When I got back, Jakob had already left for school and my mum was at work.

I made sure there was enough food in Frank's dispenser and filled his water bowl. He immediately stuck his head in it and starting lapping the water.

Adrian was sitting at the kitchen table, eating cereal and reading a comic.

"Guess what?" I said.

Adrian looked up from the magazine. "What?"

"Kaland has decorated a Christmas tree in his front yard."

"No way. Why?"

I shrugged. "Beats me. I guess he thinks it's Christmas."

Adrian laughed. "Wow, that's next-level crazy. Even for him."

I sat down at the table and ate a slice of bread with cheese while playing *hocus.* on my phone.

After breakfast, Adrian and I cycled to school together like always. When we passed Kaland's house, Adrian laughed as I pointed out the tree.

Adrian can't cycle like a normal person. He has a BMX and always has to ride in circles, jump or do a little trick.

"Check this out!" Adrian sped up and did a 360 on the pavement. A perfect one.

He doesn't really do these kinds of things to show off. He just has to make everything more adventurous and action-filled. Otherwise he gets bored.

We met up with Filip at the corner of his street and then all cycled to school together. Filip is in Adrian's class. They are both a year younger than me, but they are both already taller than me. If someone who didn't know us met us for the first time, they'd probably guess that I was younger than them.

"What are we doing today?" Filip asked. "After school, I mean."

"We can go to our house and play video games," Adrian suggested. "Jakob will be at handball practice again, so we can have the basement."

If Jakob is home he has dibs on the basement. He thinks

this is his natural-born right because he is the oldest. And even if we were to try and claim that we were there first, the PlayStation belongs to him so there is nothing we can do.

We parked our bikes outside the school and walked across the schoolyard together.

My classroom is in the opposite direction from theirs, so we said goodbye after walking through the main door.

First class we had social studies with Johannes Helberg. Johannes is my homeroom teacher and I have him for three different subjects – English, science and social studies.

We were talking about phobias and fears, and he asked an open question to the class, "What is your biggest fear?"

This is what everyone answered:

"Tan lines."

"Spiders."

"Sharks."

"Heights."

Johannes looked at me. "Sander. What are you afraid of?"

Of always being the short guy.

Of never getting a girlfriend.

Of dying alone.

I said, "Snakes."

Johannes started talking about how your fears can feel

very real even when they're not. I looked out the window. An old lady was walking by with a cat on a lead, which looked really strange to me. I thought the whole selling point of cats was that you didn't have to walk them or bathe them or anything like that. The lady disappeared around the corner and I caught my reflection in the window. My disproportions are not as severe as in other SRS cases. At least, that is what my doctors always used to say, but my head is still slightly too big. Or, it is not actually my head that is big. It is my body that is too small.

At the end of class I collected my things and made my way towards the door. Just as I was about to leave the classroom, Johannes said, "Sander?"

I turned around and looked at him.

"Do you mind sticking around for a minute?"

Now, I know I said that I hadn't been in trouble before, but even I knew that this wasn't really a question. Not one that I could say no to, anyway.

"I would like to talk to you," Johannes continued.

I sat down on a desk close to his, and he pulled out a sheet of paper from a folder. It had red marks all over it, and I knew straight away what it was. It was one of the tests I had failed.

"I've had a look at some of your recent work," Johannes said. "It seems you have been struggling a bit lately?"

I nodded slightly and he took out another sheet. My science test.

"I had a word with some of the other teachers, and it seems that this has happened in other classes too. Norwegian and maths? And it all seems to have happened around the same time, about a month ago."

I shrugged.

Johannes got a serious look on his face. "Sander, is everything as it should be at home?"

"What? Yes!"

"You've never had problems before…"

"I just failed a couple of tests, that's all."

"Well, you didn't exactly fail. As you know, the grades range from one to six, six being the best. You got a one. One is also a grade. We don't fail anyone."

"But what if you get a one in all your subjects?"

"We would get you help before that happens. That is why we are having a chat now."

"But what if you got help, but you still got a one in all subjects? What would happen then? You would be held back a year, right?"

"No, of course not. No one is held back."

"Oh."

"Why are you asking me that?"

I shrugged. "Just wondering."

He paused for a minute before leaning forward in his chair. "You think you can do better on the next test?"

"Yeah."

He smiled. "So do I."

As soon as he let me go, I hurried out of the classroom.

What was he talking about? Why the hell would he ask me about my home situation? I was beginning to realize that faking being dumb was a really bad idea. Most people would probably know that to begin with. And apparently, they don't even hold kids back, which made me feel even more stupid.

I had been thinking that things would be easier if I was in the year below me. I mean, everyone already thinks I am younger anyway, and I thought it might give me more time to catch up to the rest of the kids in my class. Height wise, that is. But deep down I knew that it wouldn't have worked. Most of them were growing past me already. It really was a ridiculous plan.

After school, Filip came over to our house to play *Dragon Ball Fighterz*. It's kind of a pointless game, you just each choose a character and then you fight each other.

First, I played against Filip, and I won. This probably shouldn't have made me overly happy, but it did. There are not a lot of things that I will beat the boys at, but this is one of them. I have never been in a real fight, but there is no question that both Adrian and Filip would be able to take me.

I remember my dad telling me that strength comes from within. But that was easy for him to say. He was a hundred and eighty-five centimetres tall and could pull a twenty-kilo cod over the railings of his boat all by himself. He was the kind of guy who no one would mess with.

Afterwards, Adrian and Filip played against each other and Filip got the upper hand right away, by pounding Adrian's character to the ground. Adrian was quick to retaliate and evened the score with a few punches. In the middle of their round, Jakob walked in with his friend Preben.

"All right, boys," Jakob said, "out."

Adrian didn't respond, because he was busy kicking Filip's character in the face.

"Did you not hear what I said? Time's up." Jakob always acts tougher when his friends are around.

When Adrian still didn't respond, Jakob yanked the controller out of his hand.

"Hey, knock it off! You are such a jerk," Adrian yelled, and he kicked Jakob's leg.

"Okay, that's it." Jakob threw the controller away and pinned Adrian to the floor. Jakob couldn't have his little brother kick his leg without retaliating, when his friend was watching.

Even though Jakob is clearly the strongest of the two, Adrian often manages to get a few good kicks in whenever they fight, because he is smart and plays dirty and Jakob is easily distracted.

Jakob continued to hold Adrian in his grip and Adrian continued to struggle.

Preben sat down on the couch and changed the input on the TV to Netflix and started flipping through the selection. Filip looked at me, shrugged, and decided it was time to go home.

I sighed.

"Just let him go," I said. "We'll leave."

Jakob looked at me. "Wise move." He turned back to Adrian. "See, Sander is smart. He listens."

He let go of Adrian and they both got up from the floor.

As Adrian and I walked towards the staircase, I heard Jakob saying to Preben, "Did you find anything good?"

Suddenly Adrian turned around, ran across the room and kicked Jakob's leg from behind.

Jakob screamed out in pain as Adrian hurried up the stairs. Jakob was right behind him screaming, "I'm going to kill you!"

Preben looked at me and said, "Do you want to watch *Inferno*?"

I shrugged and sat down next to him. I have never actually fought with my brothers. Not even when we were kids. I was so small when I was a child that I guess I just became off limits. Then it stayed that way.

Even though I was in the better position at that moment – watching a movie instead of running from a furious Jakob, ready to kill – a part of me felt left out. I probably wouldn't be able to take Jakob regardless of my condition, but Adrian is my younger brother and I should be able to beat him up. Not that I'd want to. But it would be nice to know that I could.

So, eventually the school did contact my mum. And she freaked out. She was so frazzled in the morning that she almost put orange juice in her coffee instead of milk.

"Why didn't you tell me you were having problems?"

She put the juice back in the fridge and took out the milk carton.

If you ask me, the school could have had the decency to wait until she was at work and I was at school before calling her. Then she would have had time to cool off before talking to me. No one needs that kind of drama at breakfast.

"I have it under control," I said. "I'll do better next time."

"Your teacher says that this has been going on for a while already."

"I was just distracted."

Eventually she let me off the hook, because she had to go to work. But I knew the conversation wasn't over. I sat down at the table, and Jakob looked up from his cereal bowl.

"You want some brotherly advice?"

"What?"

"Be less stupid." He got up from the table and put his bowl in the sink before leaving.

That was my own fault, really. If Jakob asks whether you want advice, the answer should always be no.

Adrian kept shooting me glances between bites. He acted like he was worried that I'd actually turned dumb overnight, and he didn't know what to say.

After breakfast, we met up with Filip and cycled to school together. Filip said that he had gotten *Strange Brigade* for his Xbox and we should all come to his house after school to play.

For my first class I had social studies with Johannes Helberg again. This time we were talking about advertising and how it has developed through the years.

In my textbook there was a milk ad from the fifties. It showed a picture of a very tall man holding a carton of milk, looking down at a small child. The man was saying *"If you want to be as tall as me, keep drinking your milk."*

"Hey, Sander!"

It was the kid next to me, named Daniel. He is a real know-it-all. I turned and looked at him.

"What?"

"Maybe you should try drinking some milk."

A few people laughed, but most people either didn't hear or decided to ignore him. It was still enough to leave Daniel with a satisfying grin on his face though. He is not even one of the tall guys. But he is taller than me, and that's all that matters.

I looked at my book again. Under the picture, it said that milk was rich in protein, vitamin D and calcium, and even though it couldn't make you grow taller it could help kids reach their potential height.

When class was over I kept thinking about all the things I should have said to Daniel.

Maybe you should learn a new joke!

Maybe you should get a life!

Too bad you can't drink anything to improve your IQ.

All good responses.

…That all came too late.

I went to meet up with Adrian and Filip. They were standing in our usual corner, with a boy I'd never seen before. He had broad shoulders and a crew cut.

"Hey," I said as I walked up.

"Hey," Adrian said. He gestured towards the new guy. "This is Niklas. He just moved here from Haasund. He started today."

"Hi, how you doing, buddy?" the boy said. "What's your name?"

"Sander."

"Hey, Sander. I was just telling these guys that I have a bike ramp at my house. We're going to check it out after school. You can join us if you want?"

"I thought we were playing *Strange Brigade* after school?" I said.

"Oh, come on," Niklas said, "you can play video games any time."

I looked at the boys. They just shrugged.

So after school we all cycled over to Niklas's house. He said he lived on Rosk, which is in the southern part of town. Niklas suggested we'd go by the main road.

"It's faster to go through the underpass and past the butcher's," I said.

He shrugged. "Okay, cool."

As we cycled, Niklas was telling us about different tricks he had done on the ramp. "Once I did a tailwhip, but that was a long time ago. I only made it that one time."

"Wow," Filip said. "That's awesome. Adrian is really good at 180s."

"Yeah, that's cool too," Niklas said.

Niklas lived in a red house with green window sills. The house looked kind of old, but it could've just been that it hadn't been painted in a while. In the front yard, there were a few things lying around – a rake, a broken sprinkler, a hose – and on the doorstep stood a pair of wellies. Everything looked quite messy, for a place that someone had just moved into.

"This way," Niklas said, and he led us around the corner of the house.

The ramp was in the backyard. It was bigger than I had expected, and the minute I saw it I knew I wasn't going to try it. On my way over I had thought that I most likely wouldn't want to try it, but when I saw it, I knew for sure.

Okay, I know I'm the biggest coward around. It's just that when I was little, things were pretty slow. I didn't learn to ride a bike until I was nine years old. The thought of falling over and injuring myself really scared me. And it still kind of does. I mean, I'm not afraid of riding a bike. Not exactly. I just don't like to go fast or cycle down steep hills or jump off ramps. I'm obviously fine cycling to school and stuff. Except in the winter when the roads get slippery. The winters are pretty mild around here, but I'm not sure that's a good thing. No one would be able to ride their bikes if there was a lot of snow, but most people don't avoid cycling because of a little frost. Adrian and I used to catch a ride to school with Mum, but a few months ago she started going into the office earlier and we've been cycling to school ever since. I don't know what I'll do once winter comes. I obviously can't tell my friends that I don't want to cycle because of the frost. Not when my younger brother does 360s on his way to school.

"We can take turns using my bike," Niklas said, pointing at a red and shiny BMX bike that stood against the wall of the house.

"I can use my own," Adrian said.

"Yeah, if you want. I'll go first. I only have two sets of knee pads and elbow pads. And one helmet. We can take turns using them as well."

Niklas went first. He didn't do a trick or anything. It was just a regular jump.

They all jumped one time each, then Niklas turned to me. "You're up."

"I'm all right, actually."

"What do you mean?"

"I sprained my ankle a few days ago, so I'd rather just watch."

Niklas shrugged. "All right, suit yourself. I guess it's my turn again then."

I went and sat on a bench and watched the others. Adrian started doing 180s in the air, and most of the time he landed quite nicely too.

I took out my phone and started taking some pictures. I was trying to catch Adrian just as he jumped off the ramp, but there was too much sunlight to take a good picture. I've read online about how to take pictures during sunny days. You need to have a white surface on one side of the person you're photographing, to balance the light out evenly. You can do this by having your object stand next to a white wall, or you need to ask an assistant to hold a white sheet of paper or reflector on the opposite side of your model. I wouldn't know who to ask to be an assistant. People aren't really that interested in photography. At least, not any of the people I know.

"Hey, what are you doing?" Niklas sat down next to me. "Are you taking photos?"

"Yeah, not really." I showed him the overexposed picture of Adrian jumping off the ramp. He was basically just a silhouette in the background, and flare caused a number of colourful circles to cut across the frame.

"Well, that's kind of cool," Niklas said. "It looks artistic."

I shrugged and put the phone back in my pocket.

Filip flew off the ramp and fell over as soon as he landed. He didn't seem to be hurt, though. He just got up and started removing his knee pads.

"So, how come you moved here?" I asked Niklas.

"My mum wanted to live with her boyfriend. This is his house."

"Oh."

"I don't know him too well, they've only been together for about six months, but my mum says she's not getting any younger."

"Isn't it a bit strange to go live with someone you don't really know?"

He shrugged. "Maybe a little. He's cool though."

Filip called Niklas to tell him it was his turn.

"Okay!" Niklas called back, before turning to me. "Are you sure you don't want to have a go?"

I shook my head. "Not today."

"All right." He got up from the bench and jogged over to the ramp.

We got home around 5 o'clock, just in time for dinner. We were having chilli, which I really like. My mum was stirring the big casserole pot and said it would be done any minute.

She asked us to lay the table, so Adrian got the plates

and I fetched the glasses and laid them out.

As I opened the cutlery drawer, my mum turned to me.

"Oh, I want to check your homework once you are done."

Great. She had never done that before. I guess this was just another grand prize I had earned for acting like a moron.

"Whatever," I said, and grabbed four spoons.

"There is lemonade in the fridge if you want," Mum said.

"No, thanks. I'll have a glass of milk instead."

She looked at me. "You don't like milk."

"I do now."

4

Growth hormone therapy. This is the reason why I am as tall as I am. At least, that is what the doctors think. I have always been small for my age, even before I was born. In the first couple of months after I was born, the doctors did all kinds of tests to try and figure out why I wasn't developing as I should and why I didn't take in nutrition properly. My mum couldn't get me to breastfeed, and I had to be fed through a tube in my nose.

Growing up, people always thought Adrian was older than me. Because, after he was born he pretty much grew past me in about five minutes.

I started the growth hormone therapy when I was four, and since then I've been taking injections every night, before bed. First my mum did them for me, but when I got older I learned to do them myself. Growth hormones don't work for everyone, but they did for me. There was even a time where Adrian and I were the same height. It didn't last.

Since I started the treatment, I've gone to the hospital for a check-up every six months. They do a blood test and measure me and weigh me, to check if everything is on track. Once I stop growing they will take me off the treatment, because it means it's not working any more.

On Monday morning I showered, had breakfast and took Frank for his morning walk. But I didn't measure myself. I decided I didn't want to ruin my day before it had even started.

For my first class I had maths, which is pretty brutal so early on a Monday, but I did my best to pay attention.

After the first break, I made my way to the science room. Johannes started class off by saying that we were going to have an end-of-term science project that would count for sixty per cent of our grade. We were going to make a working project like a windmill or an electric generator and document the process.

"We are not going to start working on it just yet," Johannes said, "but you could start thinking about what you want to do. If you need any help coming up with a project, I'd be happy to give you some ideas."

A guy named Martin raised his hand.

"Can I make a maze for my pet rat?"

"We'll talk more about the specifics for the project later," Johannes said, "but I have put up all the requirements online." He clapped his hands together. "Now, let's get class started."

He gave us a quick introduction and then he paired us up to do an experiment.

After class I collected my packed lunch from my classroom and went to meet Adrian and Filip. We normally sit on the steps leading up to the school staffroom and eat. When I rounded the corner, I saw the boys sitting on the steps, talking to Niklas.

"So, what are we doing after school?" he asked them.

Filip took out a sandwich from a brown paper bag.

"I think they're having a movie showing at the library today," he said.

"Yeah." Adrian bit into a salami and cheese sandwich. "It's one of the *Pirates of the Caribbean* films, I think."

"Okay, that sounds good," Niklas said. "Is your little brother coming along too?"

They didn't know I was there – they hadn't seen me yet. I quickly turned around and stepped behind the corner, out of sight.

Adrian sounded like he still had his mouth full of food. "He's my older brother."

"No, I am talking about Sander."

"So am I."

Suddenly I didn't feel like having lunch with them. I turned around and walked down the hallway the same way I had just come.

There are not a lot of options for places to go during lunch break, so I just went back to my classroom and ate at my desk. I wasn't really hungry, but I ate my turkey sandwich anyway. Turkey is high in protein, which helps you build muscles.

For my last class, I had PE. In PE, normally one of three things becomes clear.

I am not the strongest.

I am not the fastest.

I am not the biggest.

After a quick warm-up, doing laps around the gym, our teacher Geir blew his whistle and announced that we were going to play basketball.

This meant that, today, two things would become clear.

I am not the fastest.

I am not the biggest.

Geir split us into two teams, blew his whistle again and the game started.

So mostly I was just running up and down the court, waving my arms for the ball at the right times and pretending to care. You have to at least pretend, because

Geir will call you out if you don't make an effort.

Then someone passed me the ball. I was pretty much all alone in front of the basket, so I went for the shot. Because what else can you do? The ball barely swiped the net before bouncing outside the court line.

"Nice try, Sander," this guy named Evind said, which ticked me off. None of the other kids gets a "nice try" for missing the basket.

Eivind is the son of a dentist. He gets good grades and he is tall and has shiny white teeth and wavy hair. He's the most perfect guy in the world.

As we ran back down the court, Eivind slapped me on my shoulder and said, "Don't worry, you'll make it next time."

I wanted to hurt him. I know he meant well but that just made it worse. I can't tell people to eff off when they mean well.

I'd like to say that the next time I got the ball in my hands I scored a goal. A three-pointer, even. But the truth is that for the rest of the game I didn't even try to score. Every time someone gave me the ball, I immediately passed it to someone else.

After school, I met up with the others by the bike rack.

"Where were you during lunch?" Filip said.

"I...umm..." I pretend-coughed, to buy myself more

time. "I had to study. I have a test coming up."

"Okay. We're going to the library now to watch *Pirates of the Caribbean*. Are you coming?"

"No." I released my bike from the rack. "*Pirates* is for kids."

I parted ways with them at the second roundabout. I stopped by the shop and bought a litre of milk. I went out to the car park and downed the whole carton before throwing it in the bin. It tasted horrible, but I didn't stop drinking until I finished the whole thing. Then I got back on the bike and cycled as fast as I could.

I wasn't even halfway home before I had to stop and throw up at the side of the road.

I walked my bike the rest of the way. I was still feeling pretty sick and all I could think about was that I was going straight to bed to lie down, the minute I got home. The fresh air seemed to help though and by the time I reached my street I was feeling a lot better.

Maybe I didn't need to lie down after all. Maybe I'd just take it easy and play video games for a few hours. Jakob probably wouldn't be home yet, so I'd have the basement to myself.

When I reached my house, I dropped the bike off in the driveway. To my surprise, the front door was unlocked. But it wasn't Jakob who was home. It was my mum.

"Hi, Sander," she said as I walked into the kitchen.

"What are you doing home?"

"I told you I finished early today."

I'm pretty sure she didn't tell me that. Mum has flexible hours, so technically she can leave work early, but it doesn't happen very often.

"Where's Adrian?" Mum said, as she started going through the mail on the kitchen counter.

"He went to the library. With Filip and Niklas."

She frowned. "Who's Niklas?"

"A new kid in his class."

"Oh okay. Well, I'm glad you're here. I could use your help down at the church."

My mum volunteers part time at the church. I think she helps collect donations for refugees. Or hand them out. Something like that.

"Why?" I said. I didn't really feel like going anywhere.

"They have received a lot of donations for us to send out, so I'm going to help sort everything and pack it for shipment. You can help me carry the boxes." She got her car keys from the hook on the wall and walked towards the door. "Let's go, we need some muscles down there."

"Then why don't you call Adrian?" I mumbled under my breath.

"What?"

"Nothing," I muttered, and went after her.

* * *

Mum parked the car outside the church and we walked into the basement. An older lady greeted us when we came in.

"Oh, great, you're here," she said to Mum. She looked like she was at least seventy years old. Well, maybe sixty. It's hard to tell with older people.

"Yes," Mum said, "and I brought reinforcements. This is my son, Sander."

The lady looked at me and put her hands together. "Oh, that's great. Thank you so much for coming. My name is Agnes. I volunteer here at the church sometimes."

"Hello," I said.

"You see, I have a crick in the back. I'm not supposed to do any heavy lifting."

I didn't know what to say, so I just nodded.

"We are happy to help," Mum replied.

Agnes smiled and looked at me, so I nodded again.

"All right, let's get started," Mum said.

Lots of cardboard boxes were lined up by one of the walls. Mum and I each picked one up and followed Agnes to a room further down the hall, which was empty apart from a table and a couple of chairs. Mum and Agnes started opening the boxes and sorting the contents while I walked back and forth carrying boxes.

On one of my trips I noticed the door to the next room was left open. Inside I could see a bunch of trays and bottles and something that looked like a reflector. Like the ones you would use to take pictures on sunny days.

"What's in the next room?" I asked, putting the box down on the floor.

"Oh, we run different events here," Agnes said. "This month is Photo Month, so we have set up a darkroom in there and we will have workshops."

Mum looked up from the pile of clothes she had in front of her. "Sander loves photography."

"Oh, really?" Agnes said. "That's great. Come with me for a second, I'll get you a leaflet."

I followed her to a small office and she started rummaging through the drawers in a desk. "I know I left them here somewhere..."

"It's okay," I said.

"No, no, hold on."

Eventually Agnes found a stack under a pile of papers. "Oh, here we are. Here, take one," she said and handed it to me.

I took the leaflet. It said PHOTOGRAPHY MONTH in big bold letters. Underneath, it said WORKSHOPS followed by six different dates, and at the bottom the church address was printed. There was no information about what the workshops would be about.

"We have gotten help from a local photographer. He will lead the workshop and show how to develop photos and everything."

It definitely sounded cool to learn how to develop photos, but I wasn't sure how church events worked. Would there be praying involved? Would we stand in a circle holding hands and chanting, while waiting for the photos to develop?

"Actually, he was here earlier, setting some things up," Agnes went on. "The photographer, I mean. You might still be able to catch him. Let's check the kitchen."

I followed her to a small kitchen where an older man was sitting by the table, drinking coffee.

"Oh, here he is. This is Sander," she said to the man. "He was just asking about the darkroom."

"Oh, right." The man got up from the chair and held out his hand. "I'm Vemund."

No one really shakes hands around here so it was a bit weird, but I took his hand anyway. "Sander," I said.

"Sander loves photography," Agnes said, by way of introduction.

"Is that so?" asked Vemund.

I shrugged.

"The first workshop is this Wednesday at six o'clock. Maybe you would like to come."

"Yeah, maybe."

"It's free."

"I'll be there," Agnes said. "I am very curious to see how all this works."

Then my mum poked her head through the door. "Oh there you are," she said. "I thought you'd made a run for it."

"We were just explaining the photo workshops to Sander," Agnes said.

Vemund put his hands in his pockets. "In the first lesson I'm going to show how to develop a film."

"Oh, that sounds fun," Mum said. "Hey, listen, I've got to leave now, but I'll come back tomorrow and help out."

"Okay, no problem," Agnes said. She looked at me. "And maybe we'll see you on Wednesday."

I shrugged and left with Mum.

As I was getting ready for bed that night, I ran downstairs to get my Genotropin pen from the fridge. This is an injection device that automatically mixes growth hormone with a solvent. I brought it with me to the bathroom and put in a new needle. Then I rolled up my boxers and cleaned my thigh with an alcohol wipe before sticking the needle in.

I thought about the photography workshop and figured I probably wouldn't go. I didn't know anyone who attended events organized by the church, and I wasn't too keen to hang out with the senior citizens in town.

But a part of me was curious about seeing the development process up close. It could be my only chance to see a real darkroom.

The next day I posted a picture on Instagram. It was the one I took of Adrian jumping off Niklas's ramp in the sunlight.

It only got nineteen likes.

So I deleted it.

I scrolled through my Instagram feed. This girl in my class, Tilla, had posted a selfie a couple of days before. She was standing in her bedroom with one hand on her waist, her head tilted to the side, and puckering her lips slightly. It looked just like any other selfie on any other Instagram account. The lighting in the photograph was poor and in the right corner you could see a pile of clothes lying on the floor. It was a classic lazy photo where the photographer has only focused on one thing; making themselves look good. Things like composition, angles and lighting had not been taken into account at all.

It had two hundred and fifty-three likes.

I closed my laptop and went downstairs.

I sat down in front of the TV and flipped through the channels, but there wasn't really anything I wanted to watch.

Then Adrian walked in and said, "Do you want to go to Filip's house and play *Strange Brigade*?"

"Now?"

"Yeah, he just texted me."

I shrugged. "Sure."

When I went to put my shoes and coat on, Frank came running from his spot at the bottom of the stairs. He looked at me and wagged his tail like mad.

"Not now, buddy," I said.

He whimpered and I scratched him behind his ear. "I will take you out tomorrow morning."

This meant nothing to Frank, and he kept whimpering, hoping I would change my mind. It made me feel a bit bad, but I knew that he would forget all about it the minute I closed the door.

We rang the doorbell at Filip's house and his mum let us in. "He's in his room," she said.

We went upstairs and I could hear gaming sounds coming from his room. A voice said, "Yeah, I used to play these games a lot before, but then I got bored. I guess I just grew out of it."

We walked into the room, where Filip and Niklas were sitting on the bed playing an older version of *FIFA*.

I was surprised because for some reason it really didn't occur to me that Niklas might be there. And I wasn't sure how I felt about that. I wasn't sure I liked the guy.

"Oh, hey," Filip said, "we were just passing time until you got here." He closed their current game and started up *Strange Brigade*.

Adrian and I also sat down on the bed and grabbed a controller each.

We chose a new mission with four players and picked a character each. We watched the intro to get the backstory, but it was difficult to hear the voiceover because Niklas kept talking.

"Once I shoplifted four large Toblerone bars from the Co-op in Haasund. I just put them into my bag and walked out. They even saw me on camera, and they still didn't catch me because I was too fast."

"They only check the surveillance cameras if something happens," I explained.

"Something did happen. I stole four chocolate bars."

I rolled my eyes.

"Anyway," Niklas continued, "I could never go to that shop again, in case they recognized me."

We started the game by killing a bunch of creatures,

but Niklas wasn't paying attention and kept dying.

We continued to kill creatures for ten more minutes before finding an abandoned campsite where we could pick up more weapons and ammunition.

Niklas threw his controller on the bed. "This is boring. Why don't we go to my house and try out the ramp?"

I looked at the others. They just shrugged, and Filip turned the game off. And with that, the game was over. We had barely gotten started!

I told them that I had a test I needed to study for, which wasn't even a lie, and cycled home instead.

When I got home, Frank greeted me at the door and I sat down on the floor so I could pat him.

Mum was in her chair, busy on her phone.

"Where's your brother?" she asked.

"He went to Niklas's house."

"Oh. You didn't want to go?"

"No…" I scratched Frank behind his ear. "I'm not sure I like Niklas very much."

She looked up from her phone. "Why would you say that?"

"I don't know. He's always bragging about stuff. And lying. He's just kind of annoying."

"Well, I'm sure it's not easy for him, being the new kid. Maybe you should give him a chance."

Frank rolled over on his back and I rubbed his tummy. "Yeah…"

I knew I shouldn't have told her, because she was probably right. Mums are always right about these things.

A couple of days later, I was sitting in my room with the others, watching *Rick and Morty* on my laptop. Jakob was in the basement with his friends and it was raining outside, so for lack of other ideas this was where we had ended up. After bingeing the last five episodes of season three, we were all pretty bored.

"There really is nothing to do around here," Niklas complained. He sounded like he was from a big city and had just discovered the limits of a small town, while in fact Haasund is even smaller than our town.

"We could watch *Big Mouth*," Adrian said. We all moaned, unimpressed by the suggestion.

"There has to be something we can do besides watching Netflix," Niklas insisted.

"Darts?" Adrian said.

It seemed like as good a suggestion as any, so we went

into the garage where a worn-out dartboard has been hanging for as long as I can remember. It hadn't been used in a long time and we weren't entirely sure where the darts were.

I pointed at some shelves on the wall above the workbench. "They should be in one of these cans."

We started going through different cans and containers filled with nuts and bolts and other junk. There was no sign of the darts anywhere.

Filip started opening the drawers in the workbench, while Adrian was searching an old tackle box.

Niklas pointed at the cabinet in the corner. "What's this?"

"It's Dad's gun cabinet," Adrian said.

"Yeah, right."

"It's true," Adrian insisted. "He had a rifle. He used to go hunting."

"So you are telling me there is a rifle in there?"

Adrian nodded.

"You're lying."

"No he's not," I said. I don't know why I thought this would be a good idea, but I couldn't stand the thought of Niklas calling my brother a liar, because he wasn't.

I went to the other side of the room and got the

stepladder which was leaning against the wall. I placed it in the middle of the room and I climbed up so that I could reach the ceiling beam. I stretched my arm out and felt around until the cold steel touched my hand. I held the key out for them to see and climbed down.

I unlocked the cabinet and opened it. It contained a single hunting rifle and a few boxes of bullets.

"Wow," Niklas said. "Does it still work?"

I shrugged. "It hasn't been used in ages, but I would guess so."

Niklas picked up the gun and weighed it in his hands. Then he lifted it up and looked through the scope.

"Wow, stop waving that thing around," I said.

"Relax," Niklas said. "It's not even loaded."

"Famous last words," I muttered.

Either he didn't hear me, or he decided not to comment on it. He let his hand slide down the gun.

Then we heard a car approaching outside.

"Quick, put it back!" I said.

Niklas put the rifle back in the cabinet and I hurried to lock it. I threw the key in one of the nail cans while Adrian hurried to put the ladder back in its place.

The garage door opened and Mum drove in and parked the car while we all just stood there and looked at her, not really knowing how to act.

"Hey," she said as she stepped out of the car. "What are you guys doing in here?"

Filip pointed at the dartboard. "We wanted to play."

I shrugged. "We couldn't find the darts."

Mum looked at Niklas. "Oh, hello, I don't believe we've met."

"I'm Niklas. Me and my mum moved here from Haasund a few weeks ago. To live with her boyfriend."

"I see. Who's your mum's boyfriend?"

"Mikal Hegreberg."

"Oh, Mikal, I know him. My dad used to work with his dad. He's a nice guy."

Niklas smiled and nodded. Then he turned to look at us. "I think I'd better go."

"Yeah, me too," Filip said.

As he left, Niklas said, "Oh – tomorrow, if the weather is nice, we're trying out my ramp again. You are coming, right?"

"Yeah." Adrian shrugged.

"Sure," I said, while secretly hoping the rain wouldn't let up, as I couldn't think of an excuse not to go.

Adrian and I helped my mum carry in the groceries she had bought. As soon as I dumped the bags on the counter, Frank came up to me and started whimpering. That is the thing when you have a dog. You can't choose not to go out, even if it rains.

The rain let up once we were out, so I decided on a bit of a longer walk. We passed the football field and continued to the church.

We crossed the car park and walked over to the clearing where six round stones have been set in a semicircle. They were collected from the North Sea and put down in memory of the fishing crew who lost their lives in an accident nine years ago. Each stone is engraved with the name of a crew member. The second one on the left says Harald Dalen. My dad. He's not actually there though. None of them are. Two weeks after the coastguard found the boat they called off their search. Everyone who had been onboard was presumed dead.

As a child a part of me used to dream that my dad would come back one day. That he had been stranded on a deserted island and finally found his way home. But deep down I knew he wouldn't.

Frank started sniffing one of the stones. I yanked his lead and turned around to go back home. When we had reached the end of the car park, someone called my name.

"Sander! Over here!" It was Agnes. She slammed a car door shut and jogged over to me. She moved pretty fast for an old lady. "Hi, Sander. I'm so glad to see you! Are you here for the class?"

I had completely forgotten that this was the day the photography workshops would start. I wasn't really keen on spending my time hanging out with a church lady and some random old guy.

"Not really," I said. "I was just out walking."

"Well, you should come."

"I can't. I have my dog with me." I nodded towards Frank. "I don't want to leave him outside."

"Oh you can bring him inside, don't worry. I don't think you want to miss this. Vemund is a really good photographer."

I didn't really have any other excuses, and I was kind of curious, so I shrugged and walked inside with her.

The darkroom was lined up with three rows of three chairs, and a clothes line was hung across the room. One of the chairs was occupied by a thin man with a moustache. He was wearing a trucker cap and a fleece jacket that looked about three sizes too big for him. Vemund was standing in front of the workbench, with his arms folded. He smiled as we walked in.

"Hello! I'm glad you could make it." He bent down and patted Frank on his head. "And who's this guy?"

"This is Frank."

"He's likes photography too, huh?"

I just shrugged, because how do you really respond to something like that?

"You can have a seat, if you like," Vemund said. "We'll just wait a couple more minutes and see if anyone else shows up."

Agnes and I sat down, filling up the first row, and I had Frank lie down next to my feet.

"Is it possible to do this at home?" Agnes asked.

Vemund nodded. "Sure, if you have the necessary chemicals. And you need a room where it's possible to get complete darkness. Preferably no windows." He pointed to the sink in the corner. "And it should be a room with access to running water."

"My grandad had a darkroom," the guy with the moustache said.

"Oh did he?" Vemund sounded genuinely interested in this.

"Yes. He was from the north."

"Oh okay."

"Hemnes."

"Sorry?"

"That's the name of the town. It's in Norland county."

"Right."

I guess no one really knew what to say next, so the

room fell silent for a couple of minutes.

Vemund checked his watch. "I'll just check the hallway and see if anyone got lost along the way," he said and left the room.

"This is very exciting," Agnes said to me. "Isn't it?"

I shrugged. "Sure." I was actually feeling pretty uncomfortable, but it was too late to turn back now. At least I'd get to see photos being developed.

Shortly after, Vemund came back, closed the door behind him and announced that it was "showtime". He lined up three trays on a table and filled them with different chemicals.

"These are called the developer, the stop bath and the fixer," he explained. "They do pretty much what the name says. In the first tray we develop the picture, and the stop bath, the second tray, stops the developing process. The fixer 'fixes' the image, by removing the light-sensitive silver print, which means that it's safe to take into the light."

"You don't need a stop bath," the moustache man said. "You can just rinse it in cold, running water."

Vemund nodded. "Yes, that is a good point. A lot of people just use water for this part of the process."

He held up a sheet of paper. "This is the negative of a photo I took years ago. The images on a strip of negatives are obviously very small so you'll need to use an enlarger to get them photo-sized. The enlarger projects the negative image onto a sheet of photo paper. I won't show you that part of the process today, but if you have any questions about it, feel free to ask me later."

Without warning, he crossed the room and turned the lights off, leaving us in complete darkness. This was starting to get a bit weird. I wondered when the chanting would start.

"And now we need the safelight," Vemund said. I heard him flick a switch, and the room lit up with a dim red light. "This light will help us see what we are doing, without ruining the picture," he continued. "Any red light bulb will do the trick. Photographic paper is insensitive to these kinds of lights."

"My grandad used a bike light," the moustache man said.

"Exactly," Vemund said. "That works perfectly. Now, since there are so few of you here today, feel free to step closer so you can see what I'm doing."

The moustache man turned to Agnes and me. "Feel free to go up. I already know how to do it."

Agnes and I got up from our seats and stepped closer.

Vemund put the photo paper that he'd already prepared from the enlarger into the first tray and let it soak for a while. He had a kitchen timer to help him remember the time.

"And now we wait for the magic to appear," Vemund said.

I watched the piece of paper as the details started to become visible. It was a picture of a seagull sitting on top of a street light. Three clouds were perfectly lined up in the background like someone had placed them there.

It was beautiful.

Then he used a pair of tongs and moved it on to the next tray. This stopped the image developing any further. Then he put it into the next tray to fix the image in place.

After it was done, he hung the picture on the clothes line.

When class was over, Vemund said, "I hope to see you all next time. And if you can, please bring a Pringles tube. We'll be turning it into a camera."

As Frank and I walked home, I was thinking about what Vemund had said about the next workshop. I had never heard about making a camera out of a Pringles tube before, and I was curious. But it didn't matter, because I doubted I'd go to any more sessions. I was glad I'd gotten the chance to learn how to develop photos, but hanging out with old people in church was just a bit too weird. So, I wouldn't go back.

I probably definitely wouldn't.

The day after, I was sitting at my desk watching Johannes grade the papers from our latest tests. I wondered if he had gotten to mine yet. I hoped that I had done well. I had never been concerned about the results of tests or anything, but after I had played dumb it was suddenly really important to prove that I wasn't. Who knows what kind of questions Johannes would ask me next?

The rest of my class were busy reading a chapter about social stigma. I was trying to do the same, but it was hard to concentrate.

I looked out the window. It had rained all night. Everything was still wet, which meant that it wouldn't be a good day to go on the bike ramp. Now we could stay inside and play video games. Maybe we could go to Filip's house. I really wanted to have another go at *Strange Brigade*.

At lunch, Niklas said, "You guys are still coming to my house after school, right?"

"But it's been raining all night," I said. "We can't use the ramp."

"Yeah, but we could still hang out. I have something I think you'd be very interested in."

So after school we headed over to Niklas's house.

As we got our bikes from the bike rack, he said, "Oh by the way, I found a shortcut to my house. We can follow the main road and then go down this small street and continue on Torolls Street."

"That way isn't shorter," I said. I looked at Adrian and Filip and waited for them to back me up, but they just shrugged. "Whatever," I added and got on my bike.

The front yard had been cleaned up since the last time I was there. There was no junk lying around and the lawn was neatly cut.

We went inside and took our coats and shoes off. The house smelled a bit like an attic. But a clean one. It wasn't a bad smell, just different.

We walked into the kitchen and Niklas gestured towards the table saying, "Take a seat if you want." We all sat down and he went straight to the fridge and took out a bottle of beer.

"Whose is that?" Adrian said.

Niklas opened the bottle. "It's my stepdad's, but he doesn't mind. He's really cool about it." He sat down at the table and took a sip of the bottle before passing it to me.

I accepted and took a sip. It tasted horrible. And wrong. Like something that had expired, but wasn't even good to begin with.

I passed the bottle to Filip, who also took a sip.

"It is very good," he said, even though he couldn't help pulling a face as he swallowed.

The next time the bottle came my way, I just lifted it to my lips and pretended to drink. I expected some of the others were doing the same, because the bottle never seemed to empty. I was relieved when Niklas took the last sip and shook the bottle to let us know that he had finished it. Then he got up and opened another.

As we cycled home, I didn't feel any different. Probably because I didn't drink a lot. We were a bit worried about our breath though, so we stopped by a shop to get chewing gum. Filip wanted a drink so we walked over to the fridges where they keep the cold beverages. As we passed the snack section I noticed the Pringles tubes, which made me think of Vemund. Was it really possible to make a camera out of a Pringles tube? It didn't really matter because I wasn't planning on going back.

Filip got his drink and we went to the checkout, where we picked out a few different flavours of gum. Spearmint, peppermint and blackcurrant. And then I threw a pack of liquorice gum on the conveyor belt as well. Just to be safe. As I was about to pay my share, I paused for a moment.

"What is it?" Adrian asked.

"Hold on," I said. Then I ran back to the crisp shelf and got a tube of sour cream and onion Pringles.

After that, we each ate about half a pack of chewing gum in the car park before cycling home.

When Adrian and I came into the kitchen, Mum was standing by the stove, cooking.

"Oh hey," she said. "Sander, I want to talk to you for a bit."

I gave Adrian a quick glance. He shrugged and sped past us.

"I've got homework," he said and ran up to his room.

Then my mum told me that she had found me a tutor.

"You what?!"

I was so shocked I even forgot to worry about her smelling the beer on my breath. I just couldn't believe what I was hearing. I was standing in the kitchen watching Mum cook her organic vegetables and I was sure I had misheard her.

Mum is friends with someone who has a daughter at my school. And not just any girl. Sofia. The smartest and prettiest girl in my year. And somehow Mum and Sofia's mum had this brilliant idea that she was going to help me study.

Mum started stirring the vegetables. "Well, your grades are not really picking up, are they?"

"That's not true!"

Mum turned down the hob, picked up a sheet of paper from the counter and held it out to me. It was the maths test I had gotten back a few days earlier. I must have accidentally left it out somewhere.

"But that's an old test. From before."

She looked at me. "Before what?"

"Before…you know… Before I decided to buckle down."

"There is no shame in getting help, Sander. It is just to make sure that you get back on track before things get out of hand."

I rolled my eyes. She didn't understand anything. "I am not going over to her house," I said.

Mum switched off the hob and pulled the pan to the side. "Yes, you are. Sofia was kind enough to set aside her Saturday morning for this. She is expecting you."

The next day, after school I had the house to myself. Mum was still at work, Jakob was at handball and Adrian was at band practice. A few months back Adrian got the idea that he wanted to learn to play the drums, after getting hooked on playing *Rock Band*. And since we live in a small town, joining the school band was pretty much his only option to learn. It didn't turn out to be what he'd expected. He wanted to quit after only a few practices, but Mum said he had to stick it out for at least six months.

I went down to the basement and played *FIFA* while Frank slept on the floor next to my feet. It wasn't as much fun playing against the machine.

I should have trained Frank to play *FIFA* a long time ago.

The doorbell rang and Frank immediately got up from the floor and ran up the stairs, excited that we had a visitor. I paused the game and followed him.

I held on to Frank's collar and told him to sit, before opening the door. It was Niklas.

"Hi," he said.

"Hi."

Frank treats everyone in the world like they're his best friend and I knew he was dying to say hello, but he didn't get up from the floor.

Niklas put his hands in his pockets. "Is Adrian here?"

"He's at band practice."

"Oh, right." He put his hands in the pocket of his coat and looked at his shoes. "Do you know where Filip is? He's not home either."

"Football."

"Oh." He made no effort to leave, and I wasn't sure what to say. "Well, what are you doing?" he said after a while.

"Just gaming." And then, because I didn't really know

what else to say, I said, "You can come in if you want."

As Niklas stepped inside, Frank went and stood in front of him, wagging his tail.

"He's not going to leave you alone until you say hello," I explained.

"Oh, right." Niklas patted Frank on his head. "Hello." He looked at me. "What's his name, again?"

"Frank."

Niklas kept patting him, and when Frank was happy he went and lay down in his spot in front of the stairs.

I had never actually spent time with Niklas alone before, so it felt a bit weird having him in my house without anyone else around. I figured *FIFA* would be a good idea, because you don't really have to talk while playing it. So we went down to the basement.

I sat down on the couch. "Do you want to play?"

"I don't know. Gaming's not really my thing."

"Well, *FIFA* is pretty fun. And simple. I mean, you just push all the buttons when the ball is near you and more often than not, you'll manage to do something useful."

He shrugged. "Okay. Sure, why not?"

We played against each other for a while, and soon Niklas started to get into it.

"I never knew football was this much fun."

I looked at him. "You don't like football either?"

"Nah, not really. Too much running."

I laughed. I've always felt that football is better on the screen. You don't have to be fast or tall to play sports on a PlayStation.

Niklas tripped one of my players inside the penalty area, earning himself a red card and me a penalty kick. "Whoops," he said, "sorry."

"No need to apologize. You practically just handed me the lead." I lined up for my penalty kick and took a shot.

"Hey, your dad doesn't live with you, does he? I mean, I haven't seen him around."

The ball went in the net. I was up four goals to three.

It had been a while since I'd met anyone who didn't know about my dad. And it's never easy to know when to bring these things up. So, I usually don't. And eventually people ask.

"No. He died when I was really young."

"Oh. Sorry."

"It's okay. It was a long time ago."

I don't really mind talking about it, but the mood always gets a bit awkward when someone unknowingly brings it up. Like they feel bad for asking and don't really know what to say. Then they follow up with the standard questions – because they feel like they have to or because they're curious, I'm not sure. It could be both.

"How did it happen?"

"It was a work accident. He was a fisherman, and one day there was a massive storm. The coastguard found the boat the next day. It was way off course, and it was empty. The entire crew was gone, so no one really knows what happened."

"Wow, that's crazy." He shifted in his seat. "Sorry, not crazy. I mean, that's sad."

"Yeah. What about your dad? Does he live in Haasund?"

"No, he lives in Oslo." He took a shot at the goal and hit the crossbar. "I actually haven't seen him in a while."

It was weird, because this conversation wasn't exactly the happiest of topics, but for the first time I was actually having a good time with Niklas.

"Do you want to play *Gears of War?*" I asked.

"No, I'm not really into shooting games. I find them a bit boring."

Just then, Adrian and Filip came down the stairs and we started a new game so they could join in.

"Sander's on my team," Niklas said. "We're an unstoppable force."

After a couple of minutes, Adrian and Filip were up four to nothing.

"What happened to this unstoppable force of yours?" Adrian asked.

"We're just getting warmed up," Niklas replied and passed me the ball. "Hey, are you guys coming to my house tomorrow?"

"Sure," Adrian replied. Filip nodded.

"Actually, I can't," I said.

"Why not?"

"I failed a few tests, and Mum's making me have this tutoring session. I'm going to Sofia's house tomorrow."

"But tomorrow's Saturday," Filip said.

"I'm aware, thanks."

"Just ditch her," Niklas said. He grinned and added, "Unless she's hot."

I rolled my eyes, because that was such a stupid, Niklas thing to say. Then I turned my focus to the game, dribbled past two defenders and scored a goal.

"Oh, speaking of hot," Niklas said, and he took out his phone. "Check this out." He held the phone out to me.

It was a picture of a girl who looked about eighteen years old. She was wearing a black lace bra and panties.

"A girl I know from Haasund sent me this."

You could easily see that it was taken in a photo studio by a professional photographer. No way did he know this girl.

"What do you think?" Niklas said. "Great body, huh?"

Adrian paused the game. "What have you got there?"

Him and Filip both leaned in to see. "Wow," Filip said. "Was she your girlfriend?"

"No, but we hooked up a couple of times."

"Really?" Filip said.

"Yeah."

"Sure you did," I said.

Niklas turned to look at me. "What's that?"

I sneered, "Nothing."

"Hey, if you don't believe me, take a look at this." He reached into his jeans pocket and took out his wallet. He opened it and held a condom out for us to see.

The boys nodded as if this was some sort of confirmation.

Anyone can have a condom in their wallet. That doesn't mean you've ever used one.

I unpaused the game and continued playing. Just like that, Niklas was back to being the same old jerk.

It wasn't like I really wanted to go to Niklas's house to check out his "amazing" bike ramp *yet again* or anything. On any other day in any other universe I'd be thrilled to be heading over to a girl's house on a Saturday morning. At least, I think so. It's not like it had actually happened before. I mean, I had been to girls' birthday parties and on play dates as a child and things like that. But I had never gone over to a girl's house just to see her. And it's not like that was exactly what I was doing now either.

Under the circumstances, I definitely wasn't excited to be visiting the prettiest girl at school. Before all this I had just been another kid to her. Well, "the short kid" probably. Her not really knowing who I was seemed a hell of a lot better than her thinking that I was a moron who needed help with my school work.

The good thing was that I didn't actually need any help.

I could just go to her house and show her that I knew my stuff, and that would be it. I wouldn't need to go back.

I parked my bike in front of Sofia's house, and as I rang the doorbell I suddenly felt kind of nervous. The only reason I was there was because my mum had talked to her mum and set up a study date on my behalf. I had no reason to be nervous. All I should feel was shame. And I did. I mean, that too.

The door opened and there she was. She was just standing there wearing a hoodie and jeans. And she smiled.

"Hey," she said. "Come in."

I followed her into the kitchen.

"How are you?" she said.

"Fine." I shrugged. "You?"

"I'm great. Super excited to study on a Saturday morning."

I didn't know how to respond to that, so I just looked at her.

"That was a joke." She smiled again.

"I'm sorry. I bet you're not too happy to be stuck doing this."

"No, it's okay. It's not your fault. This whole thing was our mums' grand idea anyway. I am sure you're not any more thrilled to be here than I am."

I smiled. "Yeah." Sofia is one of the shorter girls in my year. I was probably at least four centimetres taller than her.

"Do you want something to drink?"

I shook my head.

"Okay," she said. "Shall we head up to my room?"

I walked after her up the stairs. And I sort of wished I had asked for a glass of water because suddenly my mouth was feeling really dry.

Sofia's room wasn't like I expected. It's not like I spent a lot of time picturing her room or anything, and I don't really know exactly what I expected, but maybe some white lace curtains and pink bedding and cushions with quotes on them or something. But her room was cool. She didn't have any posters on her walls like I do, but one wall was covered in vinyl records. There was an empty water glass on her bedside table, but apart from that, the room was spotless. I wondered if it was always this neat or if she had tidied it up before I came. I was guessing the first, or else she probably would have removed the glass.

I nodded towards the wall. "Cool records."

"Oh, thanks."

"Do you like music?" I immediately regretted saying that, because it sounded really dumb. I mean, of course she liked music. Who doesn't like music?

"Yeah, I don't actually listen to records though. They're just there for decoration. My dad had a bunch of them that he was planning on throwing away."

I nodded. "Well, they are cool."

"Thanks."

"So," she said, pulling a chair from the corner over to her desk. "Do you have anything particular you want to start on?"

"Maths, probably." I took my textbook from my backpack and opened it on the chapter about dividing fractions and simplifying fractional expressions. Sofia quickly showed me how to do one of them. Afterwards she said, "Do you want me to show you one more?"

I shook my head. "I think I got it."

"Okay. Why don't you do a few of them on your own and ask me if you have any problems?"

"Sure," I said. I started doing the problems. I kind of knew how to do them, it wasn't too hard, but I was finding it hard to concentrate. It was weird doing maths in a girl's room, and she was sort of just sitting there watching me do them like she was my babysitter or something. I looked at the wall behind her desk. It was covered in pictures of herself and her friends. There was also a picture of a cat. I pointed at it, "Is that your cat?"

"That's Hedvig."

"Hedwig? Like Harry's owl?"

She paused for a minute. "Actually, it's from *The Wild Duck.*"

I must have looked utterly confused because she said, "The play."

I shook my head.

"Henrik Ibsen?"

"Oh right. Ibsen." I had no idea what she was talking about. Maybe I did need tutoring after all.

She smiled. "Just for the record, I am aware that naming my cat after an Ibsen character is pretty dorky."

I shook my head. "No, it's a good name. I have a dog named Frank."

"What kind of dog?"

"A beagle-Jack Russell mix." I told her how Frank likes to sleep at the bottom of the stairs and how I was normally the one who took him for his walks. And I wasn't really feeling nervous any more, because Sofia was actually really easy to talk to.

After a while, she nodded at my workbook. "How is it going?"

As she leaned over to see what I was doing, a lock of her hair fell down and brushed my arm. She smelled like vanilla. I know that probably sounds like a clichéd love poem, where someone says "she smelled like a flower" or

76

"she looked like the first day of spring" or something weird like that, but honestly, she really did smell like vanilla.

"Looks like you've got the hang of it," she said.

I looked down at the problem I was solving, and for some reason I said, "So I move the X here?"

It was incorrect and I knew it.

Sofia tucked her hair behind her ear and smiled. It wasn't a patronizing smile. It was a *"Don't worry, you'll get it"* smile. She started explaining it again, from the top, and I nodded in all the right places.

After we were done, she showed me to the door.

"Same time next week?"

I smiled. "Sure."

My plan had been to go in and answer all the questions correctly and let her know that I didn't need her help. But then she had smiled and been easy to talk to and smelled like vanilla.

And I wanted to see her again.

On Wednesday, I went to church. It was Vemund's second photo session, the day we would turn a Pringles tube into a camera.

Adrian asked me where I was going as I left the house, and I told him I was going to Sofia's to study. I don't really know why I lied, it sort of just slipped out. Hanging out with a couple of senior citizens at church is a bit weird, though, if you think about it, and I didn't know if he'd understand. It was a solid lie because I was even wearing my backpack, which for all he knew could be filled with textbooks. Not that he would doubt I was telling the truth – I mean, why would he? But there were only four things in my backpack: my phone, keys, wallet and a tube of sour cream and onion flavoured Pringles.

I walked into the darkroom at just past six o'clock. Instead of the rows of chairs, there was a table in the middle of the room. On it was box full of tools, like craft knives and tape. Agnes was standing in a corner talking to Vemund. She smiled and waved as I walked in.

"Hi, Sander."

Vemund nodded and smiled.

The moustache man wasn't there. Maybe he already knew how to make a camera out of a Pringles tube. Maybe he had made one with his grandad. Maybe he had made ten cameras out of one Pringles tube while standing on his head and drinking a glass of water.

When the session started, Vemund told us to take a seat at the table.

"We'll be doing something a bit different today," he said. "I'm putting you to work. This is a workshop after all."

"Is Karl not coming today?" Agnes asked.

I assumed Karl was the moustache man.

"He had a prior engagement. He said he would try and make it next time. Did you remember to bring a Pringles tube?"

I took mine out of my bag.

Agnes had forgotten to bring one. "That's okay," Vemund said, "I have a spare. Now, the first thing we need to do is cut the can in half."

That's when I remembered that my tube was still full of Pringles.

"Not to worry, I know exactly how to handle this situation." Vemund took the tube and left the room. After a couple of minutes he returned with a bowl full of Pringles. He put the bowl on the table and handed me back the empty tube.

He put a crisp in his mouth. "Sour cream and onion are my favourite."

"I actually haven't tried these," Agnes said and took a handful from the bowl. She tried them and quickly concluded that they were very good. "You know, I made my own crisps once."

"Really?"

"Yes, just plain salt. But they were pretty good."

"Maybe you should do a workshop teaching how to make crisps some time," Vemund suggested.

Agnes laughed. "Oh no, I don't think so. I'm not a very good teacher." She finished the crisps in her hand. "Not like you."

I looked at them. This was taking a weird turn. Suddenly I missed Karl, the moustache man.

They started talking about all the different things you could make out of potatoes. Agnes's speciality was baked potatoes and three different kinds of mash. Vemund had made a few potato breads in his day and once he made a potato battery that lit up a light bulb for four whole days.

Vemund pushed the crisp bowl closer to me and nodded to signal that I should help myself. I just shook my head. I had come there to make a camera, not third wheel some weird date and talk about potatoes. It didn't look like we would actually get to the camera-making part any time soon, and I was wondering if I could just sneak out with anyone noticing. But then Vemund said, "All right, let's get to it."

He picked up a tube and said he would be demonstrating what to do with that one and we should copy him.

We started off by cutting our Pringles tubes in half, cleaning out any leftover crumbs. Then we took the bottom half and made a small hole in the base of the tube with a drawing pin. This would be our camera's viewfinder. We covered the opposite end with something called wax paper and put the lid back on to hold the paper in place. "The lid, together with the paper, will act as a translucent screen for our camera," Vemund explained, as we taped the two pieces back together with the hole at the bottom. Next, we wrapped the outside of the tube in aluminium foil and taped it in place.

"I can't wait to try the camera," Agnes said.

"I'm afraid you'll have to," Vemund said. "You'll need a lot of light to be able to see anything. It works best on a bright day."

"Oh, well, in that case…" she got up from her chair, "does anyone want a cup of tea? I'm putting the kettle on." She left the room without waiting for an answer.

I used the drawing pin to create the viewfinder as well. "So how does it work?" I said.

"You just hold the tube up to your eye and when you look through it you'll be able to see what the camera sees. Everything will appear upside down."

"But how do we take a picture?"

"I never said anything about taking pictures. I said we were going to make a camera, and we did. A camera obscura."

I should have known. Of course he couldn't make an actual functioning camera from a Pringles tube. And I felt really stupid to ever believe such a thing. I decided this was the last time I'd attend one of these photography workshops. I had a feeling Agnes and Vemund wouldn't miss me much.

When I got home, Filip and Niklas's bikes were in the driveway. I heard voices coming from the kitchen, and to my surprise Niklas was sitting at the table, talking to my mum.

"Hi, Sander," Mum said as I walked in. She was acting

like this was completely normal.

Niklas pointed at a plate on the table, "Cookie?"

I shook my head. "Where's Filip and Adrian?"

Mum refilled her coffee. "They're in the basement playing *War of Gears*."

"*Gears of War*," I corrected her.

"Yes, that one. Niklas said he needed a break from all the shooting."

Niklas grinned. "We are at a very impressionable age. Shooting games might not be healthy for us, you know."

"You think there's a connection between video games and violence?" Mum said. She often asks question like this. To get you to think.

"Actually, studies have shown that there is no proven link between the two," Niklas replied.

Mum nodded. Then she said, "Wait, how violent is this game, exactly?"

I looked at them. "I'll be in the basement," I said and left the room.

Downstairs, Filip and Adrian were in the middle of a game, so I just watched them play for a while. "Do you know Niklas is upstairs eating cookies and talking about video-game violence with Mum?"

They were too occupied with the game to hear what I said, so they didn't answer.

After they had left, Mum said, "I like Niklas. He's a nice guy."

"Yeah," I agreed. "He can be."

I had an upcoming test in social studies, so Sofia and I decided it would be a good idea for her to help me study for it. We were sitting in her room and she was giving me tips on how to remember the main points in the UN pact.

"I like to come up with acronyms. It's an old trick, but I find it helpful. You just have to find something that works for you."

I looked at my textbook, where the main purposes and principles of the UN were listed.

"Okay..." I said. "How about, 'I Dispose Illegal Hamster'?"

"What is that?"

"International peace, developing friendly relations, international cooperation and harmonizing actions."

She laughed. "Sure, if that works for you."

We spent the next half an hour coming up with

acronyms for the work the UN did and the things they had accomplished in the past.

There was a knock on the door and a woman I assumed was Sofia's mum poked her head inside.

"Hello," she said.

Sofia looked up from her book. "Hi. I thought you were working today?"

"I was. I finished. I just wanted to let you know that I'm going to make lasagna for dinner."

"Okay."

Her mum turned and looked at me as she waited for me to say something.

"Hello," I said.

Sofia pointed at me with a pencil. "This is Sander. You know, the guy I've been tutoring."

"Oh, of course. Hi, Sander."

"Hi."

"How's your mum?"

"She's fine."

"Good. All right, I'll leave you to it." She was about to close the door, but changed her mind. "Let's keep this open," she said, before going back downstairs.

Sofia laughed and shook her head. "Never mind her. She can be a bit overprotective sometimes."

I tried shrugging it off, but I couldn't help smiling.

I might just be the guy Sofia was tutoring, but her mum still felt we needed the door to be open.

I realized this was the first time I had met any of her family members. "What about your dad?" I asked.

"He lives a couple of blocks over. They got divorced a few years ago."

"Oh, I'm sorry."

"Don't be." She smiled. "Trust me, they are way better off as friends."

And then – because it felt like the right moment, although it never really is – I said, "I don't have a dad."

She looked at me. "You don't?"

And then I told her the whole story.

Once I finished she said, "That's really sad, Sander," and she touched my arm. Just for a second.

After we were done studying for the day, Sofia walked me to the door. "Do you feel you're more prepared for the test now?"

"Yes, definitely."

"Hey, maybe we should swap numbers."

"Really?" Suddenly my heart was beating a little faster. This was definitely the first time a girl had asked me anything like that.

She shrugged. "Yeah, so you can message me if you have any questions about the test."

"Oh, right." And with that, my heart should probably have gone back to beating a normal pace, but for some reason it didn't.

She put my number into her phone. "I'll text you in a minute so you'll have my number too."

I ended up walking my bike home, because I kept checking my phone. Shortly after, I got a message. But it wasn't from Sofia. It was from Adrian. He said to meet him and the others outside our old primary school when I finished. Apparently, they had been playing around on the obstacle course there. When I found them though, they were just hanging out on some benches.

I got off my bike and joined them. Just as I sat down, my phone chimed. It was a text from an unknown number. It said, *Let me know if you need any help disposing illegal hamsters* :)

I smiled. I tried to think of a clever reply, but nothing came to mind. So I just ended up texting, *Will do*, and saved her number.

"Who are you texting?" Adrian said.

"Sofia." I put the phone in my pocket. "Just school stuff."

"How's tutoring going?" Filip said.

"Fine."

"How fine?" Niklas said. "Do you have some sort of hot teacher-student situation going on?"

"Shut up," I mumbled, which just made him laugh. Adrian and Filip laughed with him.

"Can we go somewhere and actually do something?" I said.

At a loss for better ideas, we agreed to go back to our house. We got on our bikes and took the shortcut through the woods. As soon as we made it to the clearing, we could see the lights from Kaland's Christmas tree, twinkling in the dusk.

Niklas hit the brakes and stopped. He looked at the tree.

"Wow, what the hell is this?"

"That's old Kaland's house," Filip said. "He's kind of crazy."

"Clearly."

"He thinks it's Christmas," Adrian said.

"Well, someone should let him know it's not."

Niklas got off his bike and walked over to the tree. He grabbed the string of lights and yanked it from the tree so that the lights went out. Then he threw them at the ground and started stepping on the tiny light bulbs.

We hadn't done anything to this old man since we were kids, and it seemed bizarre and unnecessary to do this sort of thing now. I knew Filip and Adrian would feel the same way, and I was waiting for them to say something, but they

didn't. Instead they got off their bikes and started pulling off ornaments and throwing them to the ground, too.

This was obviously pretty stupid.

And mean.

I was thinking that I should say something. But I didn't. Instead, as one of the baubles rolled near me I stomped on it with my foot, breaking it into tiny pieces. Then a light came on in Kaland's house.

"Crap," Niklas yelled. They got back on their bikes and cycled away. I gave the bauble one last stomp with my foot and pedalled after them as fast as I could.

I had trouble sleeping that night. My mind kept going back to what happened at Kaland's house. Within seconds, his beautiful decorations had turned into a pile of trash.

I only broke one bauble. Whether I had or not, the Christmas tree would have still been ruined. But I still felt bad, because I should have said something. Told them to stop.

Even if I had said something, the chances are they wouldn't have listened to me. Filip and Adrian only listened to Niklas these days. I was older than him, but he was the one they looked up to – because I was slower and weaker and couldn't grow past 153 centimetres.

I didn't even notice I was crying until the tears hit the pillow.

The next day was a Sunday. Even though I hadn't slept well the night before, I still woke up pretty early. I fed Frank and got dressed so I could take him for his morning walk. Just as I was about to leave the house, I decided I wanted to bring my Olympus camera, so I told Frank to hang on and ran upstairs to get it.

That camera is actually how I ended up getting into photography in the first place. A couple of years ago I found a box full of Dad's old stuff in the basement. Some old fishing magazines, a few CDs and a couple of books. Apart from his clothes, Mum had kept all his things. If she didn't have a place for them out in the open, they were in boxes in the garage and in the basement. She once told me that she couldn't bring herself to throw out anything that reminded her of him.

The camera was also in the box and as I held it in my

hand examining it, I accidentally pressed the button that popped open the back of the camera. It still had a roll of film in it. For the record, opening a camera with a film in it is bad, as the roll is sensitive to light and you can end up losing pictures, but I didn't know this at the time. I closed the back of the camera and felt a bit shaky, because it was possible that there were pictures on the film. Pictures Dad had taken before he died.

I told Mum what I'd found and a couple of days later she took me to a photo-printing shop to have the film developed. The lady in the shop was very talkative and asked questions about the vintage camera and I mentioned that I noticed the film when I opened the back. She explained that some or all of the shots might be ruined, but the only way to find out was to develop them.

When I got the pictures back a week later, I felt pretty nervous, because I could possibly get a little piece of Dad back. A piece I didn't even know was missing. Unless I had ruined it all by opening the camera. As I took the pictures out of the envelope, my heart started beating faster and my hands were shaking. I think a part of me was expecting to find pictures of my dad, which wouldn't have made sense if he was the one taking the pictures.

There were only nine pictures in the envelope, which meant that he hadn't finished the film. The first few pictures were of us. Adrian on Mum's lap. Jakob riding his bike. In one photo, Jakob had his arms around Adrian and me. It was taken from above and we were all looking up into the camera, grinning. Dad must have taken it while standing on something looking down at us. I was about six years old in that photo and Adrian was five, but I was a lot shorter than him.

The last five frames had been ruined. Three of them were fully fogged (completely black) so I had no idea what was in them. Two of them were partly fogged, but viewable. One was taken at a building site during a sunset featuring the silhouette of a construction crane against the orange sky. It was such an odd thing to take a picture of. What was even more weird was that it looked kind of beautiful. At least, it would have been without the fogging.

I put the pictures back in the envelope and asked Mum if I could have a new film for the camera.

And that's how I first got into photography. I don't really use the analogue camera too often because it's pretty expensive to buy films and develop them.

I put the camera in my backpack along with my keys, wallet and an extra hoodie in case I got cold. I didn't know what I wanted to take a picture of. The plan was just to walk in a random direction and stop and take a picture if I felt inspired.

Frank and I passed this little playground at the end of my street, where a magpie was sitting on top of the seesaw. I thought it was an excellent image, but some older kids were hanging out on the benches, so I just kept going. I would have felt silly stopping and taking pictures while they were watching.

We continued to the end of my street and rounded the corner. Frank kept pulling towards the woods, as this is where we usually go. I didn't really feel like going past Kaland's place after what had happened the day before, but Frank insisted, so I caved.

Outside his house, the ornaments were still shattered all over his driveway. The fairy lights were on the ground and there was broken glass everywhere. There was, however, one ornament that was still intact. A glass angel. Seeing the perfect angel sitting there amongst broken Christmas baubles and pieces of glass was both sad and beautiful at the same time. I put Frank's lead on the ground and told him to stay put, and took my camera out of my backpack. I crouched down and looked through the camera. I positioned the shot so that the angel stood in front in the bottom right corner, with the light chain forming an S-shape in the background. I set the focus on the angel and pressed the button.

I picked the angel up and looked at it. It seemed really

old. I don't think they make ornaments like that any more. I was glad it wasn't broken. Even though most of the ornaments were in pieces, the one thing that seemed the most irreplaceable was still there. I was thinking that I should put it back on the tree.

I got distracted by Frank who had started sniffing through the pieces of glass.

"No, Frank." I pulled on his lead and led him out to the pavement and made him sit down next to a lamp post. I decided to take his picture, so I crouched down and set the focus on his nose. Just as I was about to press the button I heard a noise behind me. It was the sound of someone stepping on broken glass. Frank let out a little bark. I got up and turned around and looked right into a man's eyes. But the man staring back at me wasn't Kaland. It was Vemund.

He looked puzzled. "Sander?"

"I…" I swallowed. "What are you doing here?"

"I live here."

I looked at him, not knowing what to say. How could Vemund live in this house? Either Kaland really had died, or something more disturbing was going on.

Vemund tilted his head. "Are you okay?"

"Yeah…I just…I thought someone else lived here."

He smiled. "Well, last time I checked, this house was

mine." He pointed at the sign by his door. And there it was. *Vemund Kaland.*

But that didn't make any sense. There was no way they could be the same person. I would have known. Kaland was a crazy town loner. Vemund was normal and nice and knew everything there was to know about photography.

Vemund pointed at my hand. "I think that belongs to me."

I looked at the angel I was still holding. "Yes," I said and handed it to him.

He took it and dusted it off with the scarf he wore around his neck.

"Don't worry," he said. "I know you're not the one who did this. It happened yesterday. I heard them rushing away, laughing and shouting." He smiled a tired smile. "Kids."

"Yeah." I swallowed. "Kids." My mouth felt really dry, and I kept swallowing.

"A few weeks ago was the anniversary of the day my wife passed away."

"Oh," I said. Because I felt really confused and didn't know what to say.

"Yup," he said. "Sixteen years ago."

Then I realized what I should say. "I'm sorry."

"She loved Christmas," he continued. "Every part of it.

She would buy Christmas presents and decorations all year round. She would bake seven different kinds of Christmas biscuits every year, because that is the tradition, and she would fill the house with smells of coconut macaroons and gingerbread cookies. And I was never allowed to have a taste before Christmas Eve."

I really wished he would stop talking. My head felt like it was about to explode. It was just too much.

"She normally did everything herself, because she wanted things in a certain way and we both felt I was in her way if I tried to help, so it was easier to just leave her to it. But one thing we always did together was decorate the Christmas tree."

In that moment, I couldn't think of anything that had ever made me feel worse. We had turned his memories into a Christmas ornament graveyard. And for what? Because we felt like it? For a laugh? It certainly didn't seem funny now.

"I was feeling a bit sentimental, so I decorated the tree. I realize that must seem strange."

"No." I shook my head. "No, not at all."

He looked at me and smiled slightly. "I know it's not Christmas."

I shrugged. "Yeah."

"Is that an Olympus you have there?"

I looked down at my hand that was still clutching the camera. "Yes."

"That's an interesting camera for a boy your age to have. How old are you again? Sixteen?"

I looked at him. It was the first time anyone had mistaken me for being older. Ever.

"Fifteen," I replied.

"Aha." He nodded. "Anyhow, it's a good camera."

I nodded.

"Well, since you're here, maybe you could give me a hand cleaning this mess up?"

I didn't say anything. I really didn't know what to say or what to do.

"Hold on, I'll get you a broom," Vemund said, and he walked over to the garage.

I tried to grasp everything that had just happened.

Vemund came back and handed me a broom. "Why don't you start sweeping the glass, and I'll throw the bigger pieces straight in the trash?"

My head was spinning, and I needed to leave. Right away. "Actually…I…I have to go."

I gave him back the broom, grabbed Frank's lead and rushed away as fast as I could, without looking back.

I had problems concentrating in school the next day. My mind kept going to Kaland and Vemund, Vemund and Kaland. How could they be the same person? I hadn't seen Kaland in ages, which made sense as I don't think he gets out much. And I guess Vemund kind of looked like the man I remembered. But it still didn't make sense. One was normal and one was crazy.

After school, as I did my homework, my mind wandered again. I kept trying to think of strange things Vemund had said or done during the photo sessions that would explain him being the town crazy. The only thing I could think of was when he delayed the second session because he got so occupied eating Pringles and talking to Agnes. But that was just a bit strange, not crazy. Certainly not Kaland crazy.

Then I tried to think of what kind of crazy things Kaland had done when we were kids and I came up blank.

I decided to ask Adrian. He was sitting on his bed reading *The Walking Dead*.

"Question," I said and sat down at his desk. He looked up.

"Okay…"

"You know Kaland?"

"Umm, yeah?"

"Why did we used to call him crazy?"

"What?" He laughed. "Are you serious?"

"Yes. I mean, what sort of crazy things has he done?"

"Apart from decorating a Christmas tree, like, two months too early?"

"Yes," I said. Adrian had a puzzled look on his face. "I mean, yeah, apart from the Christmas tree, what sort of crazy things has he done?"

"He used to run after us, shouting."

"Because we pranked him?"

"Yeah, but he was a lunatic, for sure. That's why we pranked him in the first place. Why are you even asking?"

I shrugged. "No reason. I was just thinking."

I paused for a minute, and Adrian returned to his comic.

"Also," I continued, "speaking of pranking. Why did we ruin his Christmas lights?"

"What?"

"I mean, he had a Christmas tree even though it's not Christmas. That's strange, sure, but he wasn't hurting anybody. So why did we ruin it?"

I could see Adrian was starting to get annoyed. "I don't know. You were there too. Why are you asking me?"

"Do you think we would have done it if Niklas wasn't there?"

"What?"

"I mean, don't you think Niklas is a bit...you know..."

"A bit what?"

"I don't know. A bit obnoxious sometimes?"

He looked at me like I was an idiot. "He's funny," he said. "I like hanging out with him."

I decided not to push it, and left the room. I went down to the living room and turned the TV on.

Shortly after, Mum came home carrying a bunch of trays and bottles.

"What's that?" I said.

"Oh, Vemund left these at the church. I guess the photo sessions got cancelled due to lack of participants." She put everything down on the dining table. "I offered to drop them off at his house, as he lives close by."

"Oh." I changed the channel. "How well do you know that guy, anyway?"

"Vemund? Not very well. I used to talk to him and his

wife if I ran into them in the neighbourhood." She sat down next to me and put a cushion in her lap. "Once, when we had just moved in here, they invited your dad and I over for a cupcake and jazz night."

I looked at her. "What even is that?"

"We ate cupcakes and listened to jazz records."

"So you went?"

"Sure."

"Isn't he, like, crazy or something?"

She frowned. "Why would you say that?"

I shrugged.

"He's not crazy. He's a bit eccentric, maybe." She gave me a look. "You know, just because people are different, doesn't make them crazy."

I knew that, obviously.

"He loved to chat," Mum went on, "but after his wife died I guess he began keeping to himself more. Quite sad, really."

I kept flipping through the channels. Cupcake and jazz night definitely sounded weird, but it wasn't something you could describe as crazy.

"Well," Mum said. "I should probably bring him his stuff before I forget."

I got up from the couch. "I can do that."

"Oh, well, that is nice of you. Do you know where he lives?"

* * *

It felt really weird standing at Kaland's – I mean, Vemund's – doorstep, and I kept looking over my shoulder to check if anyone could see me. It wasn't the first time I had rung this doorbell, but it was the first time I had waited for someone to answer.

A part of me couldn't help but expect some crazy man to open the door wearing a tinfoil hat or something, but of course when the door opened it was just plain old Vemund, the way I knew him from church. He was wearing a button-up shirt and chinos and looking completely normal. He looked surprised to see me.

"Sander?"

"You left these. At the church."

"Oh, right." He took them off my hands. "Thank you."

"I'm sorry about the other day. For just leaving, I mean. I should have helped you clean up."

"Oh, that's quite all right. You were busy."

"Yeah."

"You know, I actually have something for you too. Hold on." He disappeared into his house.

After a couple of minutes, Vemund came back and handed me the Pringles camera from church.

"Oh." I accepted it. "Thanks."

"You don't like it?"

"No, it's okay." I turned the tube in my hand. "I mean, I kind of thought we would make a real camera. One that actually worked."

"It is a real camera. It does work."

"Sure."

"However, if you mean a camera that can take actual pictures, it's also possible to make that. But then we are going to need a different container."

"How?"

"If you have time now, I could show you?"

I stepped inside and closed the door behind me.

The house smelled like moth-eaten clothes, and vinegar. The living-room floor was filled with piles of old newspaper, magazines and books, and the room was really dark. There were lamps everywhere, but it didn't seem like they gave much light.

Vemund led the way down a steep staircase, holding on to the banister. At the bottom of the stairs, there was a shelf with canned food and a big jar of pickled cucumbers. It didn't have a label, so they were probably home-made.

When we reached the cellar Vemund led me to a room consisting of a washer, a sink and a clothes line. A workbench was full of empty trays, tongs and different chemicals, and the two windows were nailed shut. Kaland's mysterious barricaded windows. I couldn't believe I was in the town crazy's basement. Just standing there, in the middle of his secret meth lab.

Except it wasn't a meth lab. I looked at Vemund.

"You have a darkroom in your house?"

"Of course." He smiled. "Don't you?"

The room seemed a bit run-down, like it hadn't been used in a while, but to me it looked amazing. "So, you used to be a photographer?"

"No, no. Not professionally. It was just a hobby. I actually used to be a youth counsellor. Would you believe that?"

The guy I thought was the town crazy was actually a youth counsellor. Nope, I definitely hadn't seen that coming.

"All right," Vemund said, and he picked up a green box with a lid. "We need an airtight container with no chance of any light getting in." He handed me a paintbrush. "Let's make it black inside."

I painted the inside of the box with a thick coat of black paint. Vemund said we would put photo paper in the box, so that it would work just like a camera with a long shutter speed.

As I waited for the paint to dry, I started looking through a pile of pictures lying on a shelf. One was a black and white photograph of a young couple. The man was holding a little box with a wire in his hand. I knew this was an old-fashioned self-timer. The couple were standing under a tree, and the lighting was just perfect.

"Who's this?" I asked.

"That's me and my wife."

"She is taller than you."

"She was taller than me, wiser than me and all in all a better person than me."

"It never bothered you that she was taller?"

He looked at me like I had said the most ridiculous thing. "If a wonderful woman like that could fall in love with a slob like me and not be bothered with these unimportant things, why on earth would it bother me?"

I took up another picture. It was of a young man who I would guess was in his early twenties. He had a long beard and, judging by his clothes, it was taken a long time ago.

"Who's this?"

Vemund looked up. "That is my son."

"You have a son?"

"Had."

"Oh. I'm sorry."

"It's okay. It was a long time ago. Still, not a day goes by where I don't think about him."

"What happened?"

He paused. "He decided to end his life."

"No way? Why?" It just slipped out before I had the chance to think about what I was saying. "Sorry," I said. "I didn't mean that."

"That's okay. It wasn't like in a movie, where he left a letter explaining it all, but he had been struggling for a long time." He sighed. "All the signs were there. I just wish that I had seen them sooner."

I wanted to know who found him and how he did it, but I thought it would be too disrespectful to ask, so I didn't.

"What do you mean by 'signs'?"

"Change in appearance, for one. The day before he died he cut off all of his beard. He was also happier than I had seen him in a long time that day. I suppose it was relief. Relief that he had made his decision and saw a way out."

"Change in appearance is a sign of suicide?"

"It can be, yes. Not on its own, of course, but there were a lot of other things as well." He looked down. "Imagine that, huh?" he said with a tired smile. "A youth counsellor who couldn't save his own son."

Vemund looked down at his shoes, and for a moment I thought he might start to cry. Then he pointed at the box. "Looks like the paint is dry now."

After we finished making the camera, Vemund

explained that to take a picture all I had to do was to remove the piece of tape covering the pinhole.

"Can we try it?" I asked.

"Sure. The best way is to take pictures outside on a sunny day, but for now we'll need to improvise."

Vemund placed the camera on the workbench and set up a lamp behind it. On the other end of the bench, he put an old alarm clock that he found on one of his shelves. "This will be our subject for the day." He looked at his watch. "Okay, you can remove the tape now."

I did what he said, while Vemund kept his eyes on the watch.

"The exposure time varies depending on the image and the amount of light you have available," he explained. "I'm trying for five minutes." After the five minutes had passed, he told me to cover the tape again. "That's it," he said. "There's now a photo inside that box."

"And now you will develop it as normal?" I asked.

"No," Vemund said. "You will."

After we switched the lights off, we filled up the trays with the different chemicals. I put the photo paper in the first tray while Vemund supervised me in the red glow from the safelight. After about a minute I could see the details in the photo appearing and the alarm clock became visible.

"Now you can move it to the next tray," Vemund said, and he handed me a new tong. When the development process was finished, Vemund hung the photo to dry on the clothes line. It was a negative; because the light parts of the image appeared dark, and vice versa, and it wasn't too easy to see how good the quality of the photo was.

"This is of course only the first part of the process," Vemund said. "Now we need to make a positive print from the negative, i.e. a photo."

My phone chimed. It was my mum telling me dinner was ready. "Actually, I have to go," I said.

"Oh," he said, and he looked kind of disappointed.

"Maybe you can show me another day?"

"Any time."

14

A few days later, in break, I was talking to Adrian, Filip and Niklas about the *Avatar* TV series we used to watch when we were kids.

"Ty Lee was my favourite character," Filip said. "She was the prettiest one."

I laughed, because he was talking about a cartoon character. He was also wrong. Katara was definitely the prettiest one. After a while I noticed Sofia making her way towards us.

"Are you ready for the test?" she asked me.

"I think I am," I said.

"Hey," Niklas said to Sofia. "Cool shirt."

She looked down to check what she was wearing. Her shirt was white and said *There is no such thing as part freedom* in black letters. "Thanks," she said.

"Nelson Mandela, right?"

"Yes, it is," she said, sounding surprised. "You are the first person to get that."

Niklas didn't say anything else. He just nodded, like the two of them were sharing some sort of secret.

"Anyway, I have to go," she said. "Let me know how it goes, Sander."

"Sure," I said, as she walked away.

I turned to Niklas. "How do you know about Nelson Mandela all of a sudden?"

"I don't," he laughed. "I saw it on *The Simpsons*. Hey, has anything happened between you two yet?"

"What? No. Why are you asking me that?"

He grinned. "Well, if you don't make a move soon, someone else might."

"Shush," I hissed, and I punched him in the arm, because I noticed that Sofia was on her way back.

"Oh I almost forgot." She smiled at me. "I'm having a Halloween party at my house next Saturday. Do you want to come?"

"A party?"

"Yeah." She looked over at the boys. "You can bring your friends too, if you like."

"We'll be there," Niklas said.

"Great." She turned to me. "See you later, buddy," she said before walking off again.

"'Buddy'?" Niklas shook his head. "You are *so* in the friend zone."

I had honestly never been more prepared for a test in my life. Even though I didn't exactly need her help to begin with, Sofia had definitely helped me. And I had every intention of nailing that test. I wanted Sofia to be proud of me.

The first section was simply yes and no answers, and I knew all of them. In the second half we needed to elaborate a bit more. There were a couple of questions I wasn't too sure about, but the rest went really well. I would at least get a grade five, which was better than I used to get most of the time anyway. As I handed in my test at the end of class, I felt really good.

For some reason I had expected Sofia to stand outside my classroom, waiting for me to finish and to ask me how it went. She didn't of course. I mean, why would she? She had classes of her own and other things to worry about. I was wondering if I should text her right after class, but I wanted her to think that I also had other things to worry about. So I didn't. I decided to wait until the next day before saying anything.

After school I met up with the others by the bike rack.

"Are we going to use the ramp today?" Filip said.

Niklas shook his head.

"No, we can't. It broke, actually."

"How?" Adrian asked.

"I don't really know. I guess I was just going too fast and the damn thing couldn't handle it." He laughed. "Man, I was about to do a tailflip too. Anyway," he continued, turning to me. "Your place?"

I shrugged, and we cycled to our place and played *FIFA* for a few hours.

Before going to bed that night, I took my growth hormone injection, like always, and brushed my teeth.

Just as I climbed into bed, Sofia messaged me. *How did it go today?*

I just replied, *#nailedit*. Like I was the coolest guy ever.

Shortly after, she replied: *Haha, I knew you would. Good job!*

I put my phone away and turned off the light. Then, two seconds later, I picked my phone up again and sent her a new message. *How did you do?*

I mean, it would be rude not to ask her back. It took longer for her to reply this time. What felt like forever went by, and I regretted not just sticking to my coolness. But then, after about five minutes, she messaged back – *I think it went okay.*

I wrote back, *I'm sure you did great. I knew all the answers except four of them, so I had to guess those. And I wasn't too sure about a couple of the essay questions so I didn't elaborate too much, but I still felt it went okay.*

That's awesome. Night.

I typed, *Thanks for helping me out. I couldn't have done it without you,* but I deleted it because it felt a bit too over the top. I kept typing and deleting messages, but no matter what I came up with it sounded stupid. In the end I just ended up writing, *Night.*

I lay awake sort of waiting for her to send me another message, even though there was no reason for her to do that after saying goodnight. I thought of sending her another message, but I didn't know what to say and it seemed sort of desperate. Instead I found her on Instagram and clicked *Follow.* Five minutes later my phone lit up letting me know that @sofiaberge123 followed me back.

Suddenly I was wide awake and couldn't sleep.

I got out of bed and I took the pencil and ruler out, but there was no need to find the measuring tape because the mark on the wall was in the same place as before.

Sofia's Instagram account is not the most creative account out there. But it is also not completely generic. Yes, there are a few selfies in the exact same pose that look like every other selfie on Instagram, but there were also quite a few hiking pictures, which I liked. I mean, I didn't actually press the like button. I was considering it, but her last post was two weeks ago and it seemed a bit stalkerish to like her old pictures. We had only followed each other for a day, so it would probably have been okay, but she hadn't liked any of my pictures yet and I didn't want to be first. Some of the pictures had poor lighting and they didn't necessarily have the best composition, but she looked pretty in all of them. I kept refreshing the page to see if she'd posted anything new.

"What are you doing?"

I quickly closed my laptop. I hadn't heard Jakob come

in and all of a sudden he was behind the couch leaning over my shoulder. He came around the couch and sat down next to me.

"Do you like her?"

"No..." I shrugged. "I don't know."

He looked at me for a minute. "Okay. Just remember that you can't sit around and expect her to take the initiative. If you like her, you have to make your move."

I scoffed, "What, because I'm the guy?"

"No, because if you don't someone else will. She's a pretty girl, you know."

"Geez, thanks. I hadn't noticed."

"Hey, I'm just saying – when the moment comes, if you want to kiss her, make sure you do. You might not get a second chance." He got up from the couch and walked away.

"Wait," I said. "How would I even know when the right time to kiss her is? I mean, if I wanted to."

He shrugged. "Give it time. You'll know."

That was terrible advice. He'd basically told me to hurry up and take my time all at once. I had no clue how this guy did so well with girls. I put my laptop away and got ready for school.

I did get a five on the test, just like I expected. When Johannes put it on my desk, he smiled and said, "Good job, Sander." He looked really pleased, but probably more pleased with himself than anything else. He was probably thinking that he had reached through to me somehow.

It was nice to read his comments on my paper and I knew my mum would be really happy, but I was mostly excited about showing it to Sofia.

I found her outside her classroom.

"Hey," I said.

"Oh hey," she said. "I was just coming to find you."

"You were?"

"Yes." She crossed her arms. "So?"

"So, what?"

"How did you do?"

I held my test up for her to see, and I couldn't help grinning like an idiot.

Her face turned into a huge smile. "That's amazing!" she said.

And then, without any warning whatsoever, she hugged me. It only lasted for a few seconds, but it felt like a couple of days. Her skin was soft, her hair smooth and I swear to God she smelled like vanilla.

"I knew you could do it," she said as she broke free from me.

I nodded. "Thanks to you. You helped a lot."

"Yeah, but you did the work yourself."

"How did you do?"

"Oh I did okay."

"What grade did you get?"

She shrugged. "A six."

"That's awesome!"

She shrugged again. "I had already read a lot of the material for an assignment I did last year, so I didn't really have to study that much."

"It's still awesome."

"Yeah. So anyway, about Saturday. You are coming, right?"

I nodded.

"Great. I was thinking that I could use some time getting everything ready for the party, so would it be cool if we moved our tutoring session to another day?"

"Sure. Whenever is fine with me."

"Great. I'll text you."

After school, I was sitting on my bed reading a book for my English homework when the doorbell rang. My mum was home so I let her get the door. I assumed it would be Niklas, as he had mentioned he might stop by after Adrian went to band practice.

I heard someone running up the stairs, and Niklas's voice called out, "Sander!"

"In my room," I called back.

He stood in the doorway, and I just looked at him, not knowing what to say, because of all things the guy now had a blue Mohawk. Not a full-on Mohawk where the head is completely shaved apart from a massive comb. He basically had the same haircut as before, it was just that his crew cut now was much shorter and the hair on top of his head was styled as a Mohawk. And it was blue.

I didn't say anything, as I was waiting for him to explain why he looked the way he did. Instead he said, "I think we should play the lottery."

"Okay?"

"Yeah some guy won 315 million dollars in a US lottery. That's sick!"

"You know that you are more likely to get crushed by a vending machine than win the jackpot, right?"

"Really?"

"Or get struck by lightning."

"You're making this up."

"No, I'm serious. Pass me my laptop, and I'll show you."

He grabbed the laptop from my desk before sitting down on the bed next to me. When I unlocked it, the last page I had viewed appeared – Sofia's Instagram account. I immediately closed the tab, but Niklas noticed it anyway. He tilted his head. "Stalking much?"

"What? No, she liked one of my pictures and I accidentally clicked on her profile." *Classic stalker lie.*

"Relax, I'm just messing with you. But seriously, though, do you like her?"

I suppose it's impossible to check out a girl's Instagram account without everyone around you wanting to know how you really feel about her. I guess using Instagram on a laptop might be a bit weird, but I like to look at pictures in a larger scale than my phone allows me to. In any case, I didn't feel like talking about it. I said, "We're friends." Which was a neutral statement and also true.

I pulled up an article listing twenty things that are more likely to happen to you than winning the lottery, and started scrolling down the page.

"'The chances of dating a supermodel are 1 in 880,000'," Niklas read out.

I nodded. "Which is five hundred times more likely than winning the jackpot."

"Damn."

I pointed at his head with a circular motion. "When are we going to talk about this fashion statement of yours?"

He grinned and ran a hand through his hair. "It's pretty cool, right?"

"I thought Mohawks were out?"

"I'm bringing them back!"

I wasn't convinced.

"Hey," he said. "There's plenty of guys walking around with normal hair. What if there is one girl out there looking for a guy with a blue Mohawk? I'm that guy!"

"Sure," I laughed. It was kind of strange to think about how someone would make an effort to stand out from the crowd, when I would do anything just to fit in.

Just for the record, there are no statistics telling you the likelihood of an SRS kid dating the prettiest girl in school.

It was the last class of the day, and I was pretty much just waiting for it to end. My mind drifted to the Halloween party. I sort of wanted to go and I sort of didn't. I hadn't been to a party before. Not a real one, anyway. Would there be drinking? Drugs? I thought about that horrible-tasting beer I'd tried at Niklas's. Would people think I was lame if I didn't drink?

I looked out the window.

Was a Halloween party the right time to kiss a girl for the first time?

At the end of class, as I collected my things, Johannes asked me to wait behind again.

"I would like a quick chat with you."

Oh God, I thought. *What now?*

The other kids left the room one by one, and I sat

down at one of the desks up front. Johannes waited until everyone had left.

"You have come a long way since last we spoke," he said.

"Thanks."

"You are doing so much better in all my classes. I'm really proud of you."

"Thank you," I repeated, because I really didn't know what else to say.

"However," he said, sounding a little less enthusiastic all of a sudden. "I'm afraid the tests we did at the beginning of the term might still pull your final grade down."

"But I did well on the last one."

"I know you did. But there are not that many tests left this year to make up for it. The only thing that can pull your grade up now is the end-of-term science project. You will have to get a six on that one in order for me to be able to give you a five as a final grade."

"A six?" I had never gotten a six on any major projects before. "What if I get a five?" I said.

"Then your final grade will be a four, which is still very good. I just wanted to give you a heads-up."

"Sure."

"If you want to get the best result possible, pick something good for your major project. I'd be happy to discuss any themes with you or even help you come up with an idea."

"Okay."

"You'll be working in pairs, which might help. You can team up and help each other be better, you know?"

When I stepped outside of the classroom, I bumped into Sofia.

"Hey," she said.

"Hey."

She didn't need to walk by my classroom to leave the building. Had she come looking for me?

"How are you getting along with Arnulf Øverland?" she said.

"He's all right." Arnulf Øverland was the poet we were currently working on in Norwegian class. I really had no clue what his poems were about. "He is a bit arrogant though. He's not replying to any of my texts."

She laughed. "Hey, can I ask you something?"

"Sure." *She could ask me anything she wanted.*

"I was just wondering..." She bit her bottom lip. "No, actually – never mind, it's nothing."

"No, no – what is it?"

"That guy, Niklas. You are friends with him, right?"

Niklas? She wanted to talk about Niklas? "Yeah?"

"Do you know if he's single?"

And just like that, with six simple words, my heart fell to the bottom of my stomach.

It wasn't that I liked Sofia. Or rather, I didn't know if I did. But I really didn't want her to like Niklas. Sofia was mine. I mean, obviously not mine. Not like I-want-to-lock-her-up-in-my-basement mine, but she was my friend. I liked spending time with her and I wanted to keep her to myself.

I knew that wasn't fair. And possibly even insane.

I shrugged. "Yeah, I believe he is."

"Okay, I was just wondering."

"Sure." I smiled. Or I tried to. I'm not sure I pulled it off. "Now you don't have to wonder any more."

"So do you want to go to the library? I was planning on doing my homework before handball practice."

"Actually, I need to get home. I promised my mum I would help her with something," I lied.

"Okay, so, see you tomorrow?"

"Yeah."

I walked across the courtyard to get my bike. I guess we'd found that one girl who was looking for a guy with a blue Mohawk.

Of course she liked Niklas. He was cool and smooth and good looking. And tall. The fact that he was a liar and kind of a jerk was clearly less important.

What Google doesn't tell you, when you type "Silver-Russell syndrome" into your browser, is that the tall girls go for the tall guys.

And so do the short girls.

17

I wasn't really too keen on dressing up for the Halloween party, but I felt I had to do something. So I threw on a red cape and a pair of fangs and, boom, I was a vampire. Very original, I know.

Even though I had put the fangs in my pocket and was wearing a jacket over the cape, I still felt silly walking through the streets. I looked over at Adrian, who had put on a dark-blue blazer together with a shirt, tie and blue chinos. He said he was going as the tenth Doctor Who. I had told him that he wasn't really dressing up, he was just trying to be the best looking guy at the party, but actually I was a bit jealous I hadn't thought of something similar. At least he looked normal.

We were on our way to Filip's, to pick up him and Niklas before heading over to Sofia's house.

When we got to Filip's place he looked normal too.

He was just wearing jeans and a patterned shirt.

"Why are you not dressed up?" I asked.

"Hold on," he said, and went over to his desk to pick something up. He put on a fake moustache and held up a white rectangular piece of cardboard. On it he had written in black marker, CARCEL OTTO JUDICIAL MEDELLIN and the numbers 128482 underneath.

I looked at Adrian, who shrugged.

"Come on," Filip said. "I'm Pablo Escobar!"

"From Narcos?"

"Well, no. Pablo Escobar, man. The real guy!"

I shook my head and laughed. It was actually pretty brilliant. "Is Niklas not here yet?"

"He just messaged me, he's on his way."

"Hands up, suckers!" We all jumped and turned around. And there Niklas was, in the doorway, pointing at us with a toy gun. At least, I hoped it was a toy gun. He was wearing a black hoodie and black jeans. He had red paint on his temple, which I assumed was meant to be a bullet wound. He held the gun to his head and grinned. "Get it?"

No one said anything.

"I'm a suicide victim."

I nodded. "Good one." But it was actually kind of disturbing.

"Oh, vampire," he said, nodding at me. "Very creative."

He looked at the others. "What the hell are you two supposed to be?"

"I'm the tenth Doctor," Adrian said.

Filip held up the cardboard again, but Niklas just looked at him. Filip rolled his eyes. "I'm the guy from *Narcos*," he sighed.

I laughed. Maybe I had the lamest costume, but at least I wouldn't have to explain who I was supposed to be all night.

As we were leaving, we noticed that Niklas was wearing a backpack.

"What's that for?" Filip asked.

Niklas shrugged. "Just some things any Halloween celebration needs. Shall we head off?"

As we walked, I suddenly got this hunch that the whole thing was a prank. That there was no party, and Sofia and her friends were just waiting for us to show up in ridiculous costumes so they could take pictures of us and post them on social media. Isn't that what they do to the nerds in movies? Were we nerds? None of us were really good at school or anything, but we weren't really popular either. We had never been invited to a party that didn't involve balloons and a jelly train before, and we were into comic books and video games.

Anyway, it was just a silly thought, and deep down I

knew that Sofia was nice and she would never do something like that.

Would she?

When we were on Sofia's street, Niklas stopped and opened his backpack. He held up a little flask. "Only losers show up to a party sober," he told us. He took a sip and passed the flask around. When it was my turn I was expecting the worst, but it actually wasn't half bad. It tasted like orange juice but with an aftertaste similar to what I imagine cologne tasting like. It wasn't good, but it went down. At least it tasted better than beer.

When we got to her door we all looked at each other, because neither of us knew what to do. Do you ring someone's doorbell when you're going to a party? Or do you just walk right in?

I checked the time. It was seven forty. Sofia had said that the party started at seven, but Niklas had made it clear that we needed to take our time and not show up until at least half an hour later because "Only losers show up to parties on time".

For someone who knew so much about parties, he sure seemed to be just as lost as the rest of us now. If this was a prank, everyone inside was probably waiting at the door with their phones, ready to take a picture as soon as we rang the bell.

Niklas looked at me. "Just text her and tell her that we're here."

"Why would I text her and tell her that I am standing on her doorstep. That is just ridiculous."

"Should we just go in?" Filip said.

"No," I said. "What if her parents are home?"

"Why don't we just ring the doorbell?" Adrian said. No one seemed to have an answer.

Then a basement window opened, and Sofia poked her head out.

"Oh, hey, guys. I thought I heard voices. Come on in, we're downstairs."

Now we really looked like idiots. I wondered if she had heard us. As we walked in, Niklas punched me in the shoulder. "I told you to just ring the doorbell!"

"You told me to text her, you idiot," I hissed.

"Get it together, you two," Filip said, and we did.

We made our way to the basement and we all just ended up standing at the bottom of the stairs, looking into the room.

So it definitely wasn't a prank. Everyone in the room was dressed up, one way or another. One guy was wearing a yellow clown wig and some big sunglasses, and someone else was wearing a onesie with tiger stripes. Most of the girls were wearing nice dresses and a headband with cat ears or tiger ears.

There were maybe around ten people there apart from us, sitting and standing in different bits of the room. It was a small party, and we were part of it. And it was because of me, I thought to myself. I was the one who knew Sofia.

Sofia was dressed as Superwoman. When she saw us, she made her way over. "Hey, come in and make yourselves at home. I hope you brought drinks." She pointed at a table further down the room. "There's punch on that table over there, but Birger was the one who mixed it and it's kind of strong."

I guess when you're invited to a party after the age of fourteen you are just supposed to know to bring drinks. At least Niklas had the flask, which we could share between us. It wasn't like we were planning on getting wasted anyway. Were we?

"Nice costume," I said.

"Yes, it's very creative, isn't it? I like your costume too," she laughed. "That red cape really shows you made an effort."

"Oh, but that's not all." I took the fangs out of my pocket and put them in.

She laughed again. "Oh sorry – I take it back. You really did make an effort!" She turned and looked at my friends. "Who are you guys supposed to be?"

* * *

While we were sitting there, watching the world go by, more and more people made their way into the room. As they walked in, the guys low-fived each other and punched each other's backs, and the girls hugged each other.

By nine o'clock the music had gotten louder and so had the people. Over by the couch they were playing some sort of drinking game. I couldn't exactly catch what it was about, but it involved playing cards and at certain points there would be a collective, "Ohhh," and one person would have to drink.

After a little while, Sofia came over to us. "Do you guys want to join the game?"

"All right," Niklas said. "But I should warn you, I am very good at games."

"Is that so?" When she looked at Niklas I thought it was clear that she liked him. But maybe that was because she'd pretty much told me that she did.

"Yup," he said. "I'm the World Drinking Game Champion of Haasund!"

She laughed. "World Champion of Haasund? Not sure that makes sense."

He grinned. "I will still beat you in this game."

"Okay, let's go."

He got up from his seat and Adrian and Filip joined him.

Sofia turned to me. "Are you coming, Sander?"

"I might join later," I said. "I'll just get some punch first."

I poured myself a cup from the punchbowl on the table. It had a deep-red colour and smelled like a mixture of raspberry and death. I took a small sip and shuddered as I struggled to swallow it down. It tasted the way petrol smells. The only way to get the cup down would be to drink it fast. I emptied the cup in one go.

I looked over at the couch area. Sofia and Niklas were not taking part in the drinking game – they were standing by themselves, talking. Their faces were really close to each other, and Niklas was leaning his hand on the wall behind her as he said something that made her laugh.

I poured myself another cup of punch and downed that one as well.

Then this girl came up to me. She was in my year, but not in my class. I didn't really know her, but I thought her name was Maria.

"Hey," she said. "You're Sander, right?" She was a couple of centimetres taller than me.

"Yeah." I didn't want to guess her name, in case I was wrong. "Who are you?" I said. I noticed it sounded kind of abrupt, which wasn't the way I had meant it.

"Maria," she said.

"That's what I thought," I said, and I filled my cup up again.

"You're like a dwarf, right?"

I looked at her. "What?" Did I really hear what she said right?

"Like, a little person?"

I didn't answer, because I really didn't know what to say.

"You are very tall for a little person."

That made me laugh, because it sounded so stupid. I downed my drink, and threw the paper cup on the table. "And you are really nice for someone...who's not," I replied. It was honestly the best I could come up with.

Then I walked away. I wanted to get as far away from this girl as I could, as fast as possible.

I'm not really sure who knows about my condition at school. It's not something I talk about. Ever. The kids I went to primary school with know, because I was in and out of the hospital a lot growing up. The others might have heard something, and they are obviously able to tell that something is up, from the way I look. But I had never really been asked about it, and certainly not like this.

Suddenly I felt really ill. The room was spinning and it felt like everything I'd drunk had made its way to the top of my throat. I had to throw up. I opened the first door I saw and stumbled inside. It wasn't the bathroom. It was some sort of study, but I had to throw up anyway. There was a large vase by the door and I grabbed hold of it as I emptied my stomach inside it.

When I came out it seemed like the drinking game was over. Adrian and Filip were sitting on the couch playing *FIFA* with a couple of other guys. So I guess cool kids played video games too. They just did it while being drunk.

I quickly scanned the room, but I couldn't see Sofia anywhere. She was probably off making out with a suicide victim with a blue Mohawk.

I woke up on a pile of coats. I couldn't really remember falling asleep on a pile of coats, but I must have, because that's where I woke up.

"Sander?"

Adrian and Filip were standing over me.

"Are you okay?" Adrian said.

"I'm fine," I said and sat up. I was actually feeling a lot better. "What time is it?"

"It's midnight."

We were supposed to be home by midnight. The only reason my mum had let Adrian come was because he was with me. Lucky him. How would he ever get by without me around, puking in vases and sleeping on coats?

I looked around the room and saw that people were leaving.

"Party's over," Filip said. "We should get out of here."

A couple of guys asked me if I could move so they could get their coats.

I got up. "Where is Niklas?"

Filip shrugged. "I think he's off somewhere with Sofia."

"Right," I said.

But the next thing I knew Niklas had bounced back into the room.

"Hey, losers!" He grinned. "Oh nice to see you're awake, Sander. Hey, I thought you were a vampire, not Sleeping Beauty."

Some people laughed as they picked up their coats by my feet.

"Funny," I said. "Let's get out of here."

When we got outside I untied my cape and threw it in the wheelie bin. The fangs were long gone. I had no idea what had happened to them. I checked my phone. There were no texts or calls from Mum, and Adrian hadn't heard anything either. I couldn't decide if this was worrying or comforting.

"Man," Niklas said as we walked down the street. "That was some party." He patted my back. "Too bad you missed most of it."

We said goodbye to Filip at his place and Niklas continued to walk with us, even though this was a detour to his house.

"Where were you all night anyway?" Adrian asked him.

"Upstairs with Sofia." He smiled. "In her bedroom."

"You were not in her room," I said.

He turned to me. "Okay, Sleeping Beauty. What the hell do you know about where I was or not?"

"I just know you were not in her room," I said, because I had no other argument whatsoever.

"What's the matter with you? You want proof or something?"

I scoffed. "What are you going to do? Show us the condom in your wallet again?"

He grinned. "Maybe I don't have it any more." And then, I swear to God, he actually winked, and I wanted to puke all over again.

Adrian immediately took the bait, with a bunch of *"No way"*s and *"Tell me more, tell me more"*. But Niklas just grinned and said to use his imagination.

I didn't believe Niklas for one second, but I was getting really annoyed. It was one thing to lie about some imaginary girl on his phone – lying about Sofia was a different story.

Niklas was quiet for a second, then he said, "Her room is really cool. She has all these old vinyl records all over her wall."

I stopped. Just for a second. He had been in her room.

But that didn't mean that anything had happened. Although…maybe it had. She obviously liked him.

I continued walking. Because what else can you do?

"Oh, I almost forgot," Niklas said. He opened his backpack and took out a carton of eggs. He took one out and threw it at a house as we walked down the street.

I rolled my eyes. "Seriously?" I mumbled to myself.

We rounded the corner and turned on to our street. "Hey, that's the house of that crazy guy, isn't it?" He took out another egg and tossed it a few times in his hand. "The guy with the Christmas tree?"

Adrian nodded. "So, do you like Sofia, then?"

Niklas held the egg up in a throwing position. "Yeah, she's all right," he said. "She has really nice tits."

That's when I knocked the egg out of Niklas's hand.

"What the hell?" He looked at me.

"Throwing eggs on Halloween? What are you, ten years old?" I was shouting. I was much louder than I intended to be.

Adrian looked at me. Maybe he was a bit worried, but mostly he just looked surprised.

"Oh, right, I forgot that you're so mature," Niklas shouted back.

"Just leave Vemund alone!"

He sneered. "Vemund? Who the hell is Vemund?"

140

I didn't say anything.

He looked from me to Adrian and back to me again. He grinned and pointed at the house. "Are you telling me that you are on a first-name basis with this lunatic?"

I looked at the ground. "Just leave it."

"Guys," Adrian said. "Quit it. Let's just go home."

Niklas looked at me. "Are you friends with this guy?"

I looked at Adrian and scoffed. "Yeah, I'm friends with the crazy town loner. Sure."

Adrian laughed, but he looked kind of nervous.

Niklas picked up another egg. "Well, if you are not his friend, you won't mind me doing this!" He threw the egg at the front window. The yolk ran down the side of the wall in a sticky, gooey line.

Niklas laughed. "Oh man, bullseye!" He picked up another egg and got ready to throw it.

"Stop it," I said.

He turned around. "Or what?"

And that's when I jumped him.

Niklas is obviously both bigger and stronger than me, but I must have caught him off guard. I ran into his side and he writhed in pain as we both stumbled to the ground.

Niklas sat up and stroked his arm. "Shit," he mumbled under his breath.

We got back up and before I even saw it coming Niklas

punched me in the stomach so hard I got the wind knocked out of me. I fell to my knees and tried to breathe but all I seemed to be able to do was inhale.

"Hey!" Adrian yelled and pushed Niklas. I think he hit him in the same spot I had already injured him because this time he groaned really loudly.

I was starting to catch my breath but I wasn't ready to get up.

Niklas pushed Adrian pretty hard and he stumbled back but managed to stay on his feet. Adrian put both of his arms up, ready to defend himself if Niklas came for him again, but that didn't happen.

Niklas just yelled, "Screw you guys!" And then he turned and walked back down the street we'd just come from, leaving his backpack and everything.

I looked at Adrian. "Let's go home."

"I thought you'd never say that."

After a few metres I turned around to check if Niklas was still around. He stopped at the end of the street and yelled, "Screw you!"

When we got to our house, all the lights were still on. We looked at each other. This definitely wasn't a good sign.

We let ourselves in and found Mum sound asleep in her chair.

I guess she had been waiting up for us and then fallen asleep. This explained why we hadn't heard from her.

Adrian looked at me and I shrugged. Then we went to each of our rooms.

19

I woke up around eleven o'clock with all my clothes on. I wasn't sure if the reason my stomach was in a twist was from the punch I'd drunk, or, from the punch I took. At least Niklas had hit me in the gut and not somewhere visible like my nose or my eye. A bruised face would have been hard to explain to Mum.

I reached for my phone, but it wasn't on my bedside table where I normally kept it. I threw my cover to the side and found my phone at the foot of my bed. It was dead. My head hurt and my mouth felt really dry.

I tried to recall what had happened the night before. The first thing that came to mind was me leaning over an expensive looking vase and filling it with the insides of my stomach. I remembered the girl casually calling me a dwarf, as if it was a normal thing to do. I didn't know if she was cruel or just completely ignorant. Probably both.

Then the whole thing with Niklas came to mind. I had never been in a fight before. When I was a kid, I was off limits, and I guess at some point we just became too old to jump each other over every little thing.

There was a knock on my door and I sat up in bed, trying to act normal. Except suddenly, I wasn't sure what normal was.

Adrian opened the door and poked his head in.

"Hey," he said. "Are you okay?"

"Yeah."

"I took Frank for his morning walk."

I normally get up early on Sundays to walk him. "Oh okay, thanks. Has Mum said anything?"

He shook his head. "No, she went to the shop this morning. She said she had to get painkillers as her neck was all stiff from sleeping in a chair all night."

That made me feel terrible. We should have woken her up when we found her sleeping in the chair, but it had just seemed too risky.

"Okay, good," I said. "Well, not good. I guess we're in the clear, though."

He nodded.

"Hey, do you mind getting me a glass of water?"

Adrian would normally never agree to be anyone's slave, but this time he just gave me a quick nod and backed out of my room.

I plugged in my phone and turned it on. It beeped a few times indicating that I had new messages. One was from Sofia. *Hey, sleepy head. Just wanted to check if you're okay?*

I didn't reply.

There were also new messages in this group chat me, Filip and Adrian have had going for ages.

Filip: *What the hell happened after I left you guys last night?*
Adrian: *Did Niklas say anything?*
Filip: *He called me and said Sander jumped him. And that you all were fighting!??*
Adrian: *I'm not really sure what happened.*
Filip: *Sander???*

I put the phone away. I didn't want to talk to anyone.

Niklas had been pretty mad. I wondered if this meant he didn't want anything to do with us any more. Or with me. If so, I wasn't sure what Adrian and Filip would do. Adrian had joined the fight in my defence, but at the same time both him and Filip seemed much more interested in hanging out with Niklas these days.

Suddenly I realized that I had forgotten to take my injections the night before, and I cursed under my breath.

I pulled the covers over my head and decided to stay there. Being short doesn't matter if you never leave your bed.

A few minutes later Adrian came back with a glass of water and I gulped it all down in one go. "Thanks," I said.

"Are you okay?"

"You asked me that already."

"Are you?"

"I'm fine."

"How did you know that guy's name, anyway?"

"Who?"

"That guy. Kaland?"

"I don't know." I shrugged. "I saw it on his postbox once."

"Why were you so angry?"

"I was drunk. And stupid. And Niklas…I mean, who throws eggs at people's houses anyway?"

"That made you want to fight him?"

I shrugged. Actually, the way he'd talked about Sofia had made me want to fight him. She was funny and smart and a good friend. She wasn't someone for Niklas to use in his bragging stories.

Sofia was mine. Except she wasn't.

By the time my mum got back, I had taken a shower, eaten a loaf of bread with Nutella and fed Frank.

"Did you have a good time last night?" she asked.

"Yeah."

"Good, I'm glad you had fun." Then she started putting away the groceries she'd bought and put four fillets of organic chicken on the counter.

My headache was gone. I felt fine. Except I didn't, because I kept wincing every time I thought about anything that had happened the previous evening. No one knew that I had been sick, but a lot of people had seen me sleeping on the floor.

I wondered how Sofia would react to hearing about the fight. It was pretty clear whose side she'd be on. Niklas was a jerk, but he was funny, and tall and cool and sometimes a very nice jerk.

When I woke up the next morning, I felt cold. I looked out the window but couldn't see any sign of frost. I checked the temperature on my phone. It said it was two degrees, which meant cycling to school should be okay.

It's hard to explain why I'm so afraid of falling.

I remember one winter when Jakob was about ten years old, him and his friends challenged each other to ride their bikes down a steep hill. They were going as fast as they could and whoever reached the bottom first won. Jakob had hit his brakes just as he reached an icy part of the road. He flew over the handlebars and broke his arm. If I told this story to a school psychiatrist, they might conclude that this was the origin of my fears.

My mum took him to the hospital and he had to wear a cast for a few weeks. I remember thinking the cast was kind of cool. When he came home from school the first day after his accident, it was covered in greetings from his friends and colourful flowers and hearts from girls. The cast seemed to make him even more popular and I kind of wanted one myself. But obviously not enough to actually risk getting an injury. But all in all, I don't remember this incident being too dramatic so I'm not sure it's relevant.

I once read an article by an academic, saying it was important for a child's development to climb trees and fall down, because this was how they learned to get back up. I was nine when I started riding a bike. Maybe a school psychiatrist actually would say that this is the reason why I'm so careful about cycling. By that time, I was so afraid of falling, because I'd never done it before, and I guess I never got used to it.

I don't know. My school doesn't even have a psychiatrist.

I got up and took a quick shower before breakfast. Then Adrian and I met up with Filip, like usual. Neither of us said much as we cycled to school. Before class had even started, two people had already called me Sleeping Beauty and one person (who I didn't even remember seeing at the party) called me "snooze jacket". Whatever that meant. I don't think I'd ever been more relieved when class began and everyone settled down.

My Norwegian teacher started the day off by talking about symbolism in poetry. And I listened, because it actually felt really good to have something else to occupy my mind with.

At break I went to meet up with the boys. I was a bit worried about seeing Niklas, because I didn't know if he was still mad. But to my relief he wasn't in school.

"Is he sick?" I asked.

"Haven't heard from him," Filip said. Then he looked at Adrian and me. "So are you going to tell me what the hell happened?"

I let Adrian tell the story, but he didn't really go into detail and Filip kept asking questions.

"It was just a stupid fight," I said. "No big deal." I didn't even know if that was true.

When school was finished, Sofia stopped by my classroom. "Hey," she said. "What's up?"

"Not much."

"You didn't reply to my text yesterday."

"Oh right, sorry. I forgot. I wasn't feeling too well."

"Yeah, I get that. So, do you want to come to my place right after school, or will you come round later?"

I looked at her blankly.

She sighed. "You didn't forget, did you?"

Suddenly it dawned on me. As she had wanted time to get everything ready for the party on Saturday, we'd agreed to meet up on Monday instead. The last thing I wanted right now was to go to her house. But I couldn't think of any excuses. "Of course not," I said.

"So?"

"Yeah, we'll go to your house after school."

I wondered if Niklas had told Sofia about our fight, but she didn't mention it. If he had told her his version of the story, I figured she would have asked me about it and maybe even been mad at me, but she didn't say anything and she didn't seem mad. Should I tell her my version of what happened?

I was in her room. Sat in the same chair, at the same desk, reading up on socialism. Or trying to. Everything was the same, but at the same time it wasn't. Because Niklas had been in this room. He had sat in this chair, he had looked at her records. He had probably been in her bed. And done stuff. With Sofia. Which may or may not have involved a condom.

"Did you talk to Niklas today?" Sofia suddenly asked.

I shook my head.

"So you don't know why he wasn't in school?"

"No, sorry. Why?"

"It's just…" She paused, rolling a pencil between her index finger and thumb. "I mean, I haven't talked to him since Saturday. I texted him yesterday, but he didn't respond."

"Really?" I didn't know what else to say.

She looked at me. "What does that mean?"

"I don't know."

"So, he hasn't said anything to you?"

I shook my head.

She held my eyes for a minute before turning back to her book. I wasn't sure if she believed me, but she didn't ask any more questions.

I turned the page over, even though I hadn't finished reading. I was meant to answer some questions from the chapter, but I had no idea what it was about.

"It means he's over it, doesn't it?" Sofia said quietly.

"What, who?"

"Don't play dumb."

"I'm not! I mean…I don't know. Like I said, I haven't talked to him."

She looked at me. "Well, you're a guy. Would you just ignore texts from a girl you like?"

The only girl I'd ever sort of liked was her. But I couldn't tell her that. I thought for a while. "Maybe," I said. "Maybe some guys really are just after one thing."

She flinched. "What?"

"Nothing." Suddenly I felt really warm. "Sorry, I

shouldn't have said that."

"Not that it's any of your business," she said in a harsh tone, "but we didn't do that 'one thing'."

"Oh. Sorry." And I couldn't help but feel relieved.

"Wait… Did he tell you that we did?"

"No. I mean, not exactly."

"Well, what exactly did he tell you?"

He said you have nice tits. And that he no longer has a condom in his wallet.

I shook my head.

"He didn't say anything. I guess I just assumed." I wasn't sure why I didn't tell her. It just seemed like I was the one she'd get mad at, not Niklas.

"I don't assume things about your sex life, Sander. Maybe you shouldn't go around assuming things about me either."

I looked down in my book, and felt my cheeks burning. Did that mean she thought I had a sex life? Or did it just mean that she didn't assume anything either way? I kept reading the same sentences over and over, because nothing would stick.

After a while, Sofia broke the silence. "Did you know that someone threw up in my mum's Grenoble vase?"

I looked at her. "What, really?"

"Yeah. I mean, who does that?"

I shrugged. "Beats me." I opened my notebook and really, really hoped my fangs had not been at the bottom of that vase.

I was relieved to leave Sofia's house once the session was over. The mood had gotten pretty awkward, and I just wanted to get out of there. It was already dark out even though it was only around five o'clock. The roads seemed slippery in places so I decided to walk my bike to have more control.

I walked through the woods to get home and I saw Vemund standing outside his house, filling up the bird feeders hanging from one of his trees. I raised my hand when he saw me, and he waved back.

"Hello, young man," he said as I approached. "It's getting harder for the birds to find food, now that the ground freezes over at night. Have to make sure to top their feeders up."

I nodded.

"What are you up to?" he said. "I could show you the next

step of the pinhole development now, if you're not busy."

"Sure," I said. I hid my bike in the bushes so it wouldn't be visible from the street and followed Vemund inside. If Adrian walked by and saw my bike in the driveway, it would be slightly hard to explain.

The darkroom looked completely unchanged since last time, the negative of the tree still hanging from the clothes line.

I noticed a stack of photographs on a shelf. On top was a picture of a much younger version of Vemund and a little boy in a rowing boat. Between them lay a fish. It might have been a trout. I wasn't sure.

At my house there is a framed picture of six-year-old me holding a fishing rod with the tiniest fish in the world on the end of it. My first catch. Actually, I'm pretty sure it was my only catch. I'm smiling in the picture, but I remember that I was miserable all day. We had been out for hours and I was cold and wet and all I wanted was to go home. The only good thing about that day is how happy and proud my dad was.

"My dad was a fisherman," I blurted out, without really knowing why.

Vemund nodded. "I know. He once brought me a thirteen-kilo cod. Said his freezer was full." He smiled. "Not everyone around here has always taken a liking to me. They're afraid of anyone who's different. But your dad was very kind."

I looked at him. I felt bad again. I was one of the people who used to think he was weird and crazy just because he was a bit different, and he was neither of those things. I had forgotten that he sort of knew my dad. "I was never into fishing," I said, because I didn't really know what else to say.

"That's okay."

"Was your son into photography?"

He smiled. "No, that wasn't his thing at all."

"Did that upset you?"

"Not really. He liked some of the same things as me, like books and music, which I enjoyed sharing with him. And then he had his own interests, like board games. He was a really good chess player, actually."

I thought about this. My dad had been a fisherman with three sons who couldn't care less about fishing. He kept trying to encourage us to get into it, but we were just not interested. If my dad was still around we could have shared photography instead.

"All you ever want as a dad is for your child to be happy and healthy," Vemund said. "My boy was neither the day he died, but I hold on to the hope that at some points in his life, he was both."

"I'm sure he was."

He nodded. Then he clapped his hands together. "All right, let's get started." He pulled a pair of glasses out of his breast pocket and put them on his nose. "Okay, now we'll make a positive print from the negative. Otherwise known as a photograph."

He unclipped the negative from the clothes line. "We are going to use a photo enlarger for the next part."

"But the negative is already photo-sized. Why do we need to enlarge it?"

"We don't have to do anything about the size in this case. We are simply using the enlarger to produce a photographic print from the negative." He turned off the main lights and switched on the safelight. Then he walked me over to some sort of projector at the other end of the room and handed me a new sheet of photo paper.

"First you place this on the baseboard," he said tapping a plate at bottom of the enlarger. "And you have to make sure the emulsion side is facing up. Then you put the negative on top of the photo paper with the emulsion side down."

I did what he told me to do.

"Great. Now we need to make sure everything stays in place," Vemund said as he put a glass plate on top of the negative. "The process would work without the glass as well, it's just to make sure everything is pressed down and doesn't move anywhere." He switched the projector on.

"The light will pass through the lighter areas of the negative and transfer to the paper underneath. When developed, the light areas will become dark."

"What about the dark areas of the negative?"

"They block the light, so, when transferred to the paper, they will appear light." He smiled. "It's magic."

After a while he turned the projector off and switched the main light back on. The colours, like Vemund had explained, had been inverted.

"It looks like a real photo," I said.

"It is a real photo," Vemund said, which I should have known he would say.

"You can see it's a bit too dark, which means I held it under the lamp too long. There are no definite answers to these things, it's a trial and error kind of thing. But as long as you have the negative, you can make as many positive images as you want. So if you wanted you could make another print using less exposure time."

He put the positive image through the same process I had done with the negative – developer, fixer and stop bath – rinsed it and hung it up on the clothes line.

I looked at the picture. He was right. It was magic. Then I had the best idea I've possibly ever had.

"Hey, if I wanted to do this for a school project, do you think I could develop the photos here?"

"Of course. You're welcome to use the darkroom any time."

"Thanks!"

"Do you want the pinhole camera as well? I still have it somewhere."

"No, that's okay. I think I have to make it myself for it to count."

"Okay, well let me know if you need any help at all."

"Actually, I could use a reminder on how to make the camera." I opened my backpack, took out my notebook and wrote down all the instructions.

Before I left he gave me a stack of photo paper. "You'll need these."

The next day Niklas was in school, but I didn't talk to him. He was hanging out with Sofia all day, so I guess whatever had been going on between them was back on. From where I was standing I couldn't hear what they were saying, but I could see that he made her laugh and she touched his arm. Just for a second. Or a few weeks – I can't remember.

This is what you need to make a pinhole camera:

- A container with a lid (for example, a shoebox). The interior of the box needs to be dark to avoid reflection of light. If you don't have a dark box you can paint it.
- A needle, nail or pin to make a hole with. (The hole will work as the camera lens.)
- A craft knife (a pair of scissors can be useful too).
- Black tape.
- Glue.
- Aluminium can.
- Fine emery paper or sandpaper.

This is how you do it:
1) Cut out a metal rectangle from the can

(approximately 3 x 4 cm). Poke a hole in the middle with a needle and sand both sides smooth.

2) With the craft knife, cut a small square opening in the box for the pinhole plate to go in.

3) Tape the pinhole inside the box, behind the square opening.

4) On the outside of the box, cover the hole with a piece of black tape. (This will work as the shutter.)

5) Tape a sheet of photo paper inside the box, on the side across from the pinhole. (IMPORTANT: THIS MUST BE DONE IN COMPLETE DARKNESS OR THE PHOTO PAPER WILL BE RUINED!)

I was standing in my garage, having a go at my very own pinhole camera. I touched the shoebox in front of me gently with my finger to check if the paint was dry. It was still a bit sticky, so I decided to wait a few more minutes.

The sound of the garage door startled me, and I turned around and saw Adrian's sneakers appearing in the gap as the door opened.

"What are you doing?" he said as he walked in.

"I'm making a camera."

"What?"

"I'm thinking of doing it for my science project, so I'm testing how to do it."

"Wow," Adrian said. "You really are taking your school work seriously these days."

I laughed.

"So how does it work?"

I didn't really feel like explaining it all to him in detail – it wasn't like he was actually interested in this stuff. "Light travels through the aperture and projects an upside-down image onto photo paper on the other side of the box. Simple, really."

He frowned. "It doesn't sound simple." He walked to the end of the garage to get his bike. "I'm heading over to Filip's. Do you want to come?"

I didn't want to tell him that I'd rather stay and finish making a camera instead of playing video games at our friend's house. It just sounded weird. So I shrugged. "Sure," I said and went to get my bike.

I hadn't expected there to be anyone else at Filip's. And I especially hadn't expected this particular group of people to be there. We walked into Filip's living room and the first person I saw was Niklas.

Sure, I could have guessed that he'd be there, but I didn't. And normally it would be okay, but I hadn't talked to him since our fight, so seeing him now felt awkward.

Sofia was sitting next to him, which I suppose also made sense. On the other end of the couch were two more people who I didn't actually know. One guy named Christopher, I think, and next to him a girl I didn't know the name of.

Filip was sitting in a chair, holding a remote in his hand and flipping through YouTube videos on the TV.

The only space available for Adrian and me to sit was in the middle of the couch, filling the gap between the girl, Christopher, Sofia and Niklas, which didn't make things less awkward.

I looked at Niklas.

"Hey," I said.

"Hey," Niklas said and nodded. There were a few seconds of painful silence before he grinned and said, "What's up, Sleeping Beauty?"

And I laughed. Because just like that, everything was back to normal.

We sat and watched funny YouTube clips. They were mostly of people falling over. And cats falling over. No one really said anything, everyone was just busy on their phones. Every now and then Christopher would look up from his phone and say, "Play that one, that one is good" or "Skip that one, it's crap", but apart from that everyone was quiet.

When we came back I went straight into the garage to finish my camera. The paint was completely dry. I had already cut out a square from the aluminium can and now I needed a pinhole. I reached into one of the cans filled with nuts and nails, to find something small enough to use.

That's when I noticed something was missing.

The key to the gun cabinet was gone.

I tried to open the gun cabinet, but it was locked. I peeked through the venting holes, but it was hard to see anything and I couldn't tell if the rifle was there or not. Most likely it was there. Adrian had probably put the key back in its proper place.

Except he hadn't. I stood on the stepladder and felt the ceiling beam with my hand, but the key wasn't there. Maybe he had put it somewhere else?

Adrian was sitting on a beanbag chair in the basement, reading *The Walking Dead*.

"Hey," I said. "Have you seen the key to the gun cabinet?"

He looked at me. "No, why?"

I shrugged. "I can't find it."

"Oh, wait, I know where it is."

"Really, where?"

"That time we were showing Niklas and Filip the gun. You threw it in one of the cans with nails and screws."

"It's not there."

"Wait – why do you need the gun anyway?"

"What? I don't need the gun. I was just wondering where the key was."

"Are you saying it's missing?"

"No, I'll go check again. I'm sure it's in one of the cans."

It wasn't in any of the cans.

I knew exactly which can I had put it in and still I emptied the contents in all the cans on the shelf. Nuts, bolts, screws and nails fell out onto the counter, but no key. It wasn't there.

I took Frank for a walk and stopped by Filip's house. He was getting ready for football practice.

"What's up?" he said. "I'm sort of in a hurry. Coach will kill me if I'm late again."

"Don't worry, I won't keep you. I just have a random question for you."

"Okay?"

"You know the gun cabinet in my garage?"

"Yeah?"

"You don't happen to have the key to it, do you?"

"What? No!"

I smiled. "That's what I thought."

The only other person who knew the key had been in that can was Niklas. He probably didn't know where it was either, but I had to ask him. I rounded the corner of my street and walked towards the woods. I could see Vemund standing in his front yard, putting up a black and white chequered flag. It looked like the ones they use in car races. I walked over to him and asked what he was doing.

"The Chess World Cup will start soon. I need to show my support for Magnus Carlsen."

I had never heard about anyone celebrating something like that. "Is that not a car racing flag?" I said.

"Yeah, but it looks like a chessboard, doesn't it?"

"Sure."

"My son loved chess. Did I tell you he played in local tournaments?"

"I don't think so."

"He was good. During one tournament he decided not to shave until he lost a game. He was a bit superstitious and thought that shaving would ruin his lucky streak. I guess it worked, because he kept winning." He laughed. "That's how he ended up with such a long beard."

"But then he shaved it."

"Yes."

"Because he was planning on ending things?"

"Maybe." He shrugged. "I'll never know all the answers."

As Frank and I walked home, I was thinking about Vemund's son. I regretted bringing up the suicide, but I couldn't quite understand how changing your appearance could be a warning sign. Everyone shaves their beard and cuts their hair. They're such normal things to do, so how could one know if it was something to worry about?

I hoped Vemund didn't feel bad not picking up on that sign – because who would?

When we got home, I took the lead off Frank and filled up his water bowl.

And suddenly something clicked.

And my heart almost stopped.

Because I knew where the gun was.

I threw open the door and started running down the street. I should have seen the signs sooner. I mean, who dresses up as a suicide victim for Halloween? I cut the corner and crossed the street without checking for cars. Oh God, what if I was too late?

Without stopping, I pulled my phone out of my pocket and called Niklas. There was no answer. As I was running up the long hill towards Rosk, I was tired and I felt sick, but I kept running. I couldn't stop. I kept calling him, but he didn't answer.

I reached his house, ran up the steps to the front door and rang his doorbell several times before knocking. Actually, I was pounding on the door with my fist until my knuckles got sore.

No answer. There was a window next to the door, and I peeked inside. I couldn't see anyone, but the light was on so I figured someone had to be home.

I ran around the house and into the backyard. I remembered Niklas had said his window was on the second floor facing the yard. I found some rocks and threw them at the window, hoping he would hear me.

He might not even be in his room. He could be anywhere. Was I too late?

I found a bigger rock and threw it as well. It hit the window with a loud thump.

Then, just as I was about to give up, I saw movement in the curtains. Niklas opened the window.

"What the hell, man? Are you trying to break my window?"

I'd never thought seeing his blue head of hair would make me so happy. I started laughing – I couldn't help it, I was just so relieved.

"What's the matter with you?" He frowned. "What's so funny?"

Then the other side of the curtain was pulled to the

side and another head appeared in the window. I stopped laughing.

It was Sofia.

Suddenly I felt really dumb. At least they seemed to be fully dressed.

"Sander?" she said. "What are you doing here?"

"That's what I'm wondering," Niklas said.

"Umm," I said. "I need to talk to you, Niklas."

"I'm kinda busy right now," he replied, grinning.

"Please," I said. "I really need to talk to you."

He looked at Sofia, who shrugged. "All right, I'll come down."

A minute later, he appeared around the corner of the house, and we sat down on the porch steps. In the middle of the yard, where the ramp used to be, was a pile of wood. "What's up?" Niklas said.

"So, I just wanted to ask you something. The key to the gun cabinet is missing."

He frowned. "So?"

"So, I was wondering if you might know where it is."

"Are you accusing me of stealing, Sander?"

"No, of course not. I just thought maybe you borrowed it."

He frowned. "Why would I borrow the key to a gun cabinet in your garage?"

"Look, I'm sorry about what happened and the fight we had and everything. Are we cool?"

"Of course we are. It's not like we violated the bro code or anything. If we were fighting about a girl, for example, the code might have taken a hit, but it's cool."

"'Bro code', really?"

"Yeah, you know – no matter what we have each other's backs. If you need to borrow some cash, I got you. If I call you in the middle of the night and need help burying a dead body, you'll bring the shovel."

I frowned.

"Or something less extreme. But you know what I mean. We're bros."

"Okay, well. I just wanted to make sure you were okay. I was worried you might…do something."

"Like what? Shoot you?" He laughed. "Oh my God, is that what you thought?"

"No, not exactly. I was worried you might do something…to yourself."

"What?" He laughed again. "Why would I do that?"

"I don't know."

He looked at me like I was insane and suddenly I felt really dumb. Obviously a new hairdo didn't have to mean he was suicidal. I guess the missing key just made me panic.

We sat in silence for a while. A large vine had wrapped its stems around the porch fence and looked like it was attacking the house. I kind of wanted to take a picture of it, but it didn't seem appropriate at the time.

"So, I guess, the blue hair worked," I said. "With the girls I mean."

"Told you," he smirked.

"You like her, right? Sofia?"

"She's cool."

"No, I mean, you really like her?"

He shrugged. "Yeah, I like her. Speaking of, I better get back inside. She must be wondering where I am."

I wondered what Niklas would tell Sofia. Now the whole thing just felt so silly.

When I got home I took a flashlight and held it towards the venting holes in the cabinet. The rifle was there, right in its place.

I had made a huge fuss about nothing. I should have felt relieved, but I just felt stupid.

Before I went to bed I decided to measure myself, because the day couldn't really get any worse.

24

I was sitting in Sofia's room trying to focus on simplifying fractions, but it was hard because my mind was all over the place. I wondered if Niklas had told Sofia that I had hurried over to his house thinking he had a gun. He probably had. It seemed like something you would tell your girlfriend. And they had probably been laughing about how dumb I'd been. Everything felt different after they started going out. I really wished I could stop obsessing about what the two of them were doing or talking about.

I looked at Sofia. She was being very quiet, and I couldn't tell if she was quiet because she was concentrating, or if she just didn't want to talk, but I found the silence uncomfortable.

"How are you doing with the homework?" I tried.

"Hmm? Yeah, good." She didn't even look up from her notebook.

There were some new pictures on the wall. Her and one of her friends dressed up in their Halloween costumes. There was also a picture of her cat wearing a Batman cape and looking rather miserable. "Shouldn't she be Catwoman?" I said.

She didn't answer.

I pointed at the picture with my pencil. "That's Batman."

Sofia looked up from her book. "Sander, can I ask you something?"

"Sure." She sounded serious and suddenly I preferred the silence.

"On Wednesday, you know, at Niklas's house?"

That was the day I'd been over there. I nodded.

"Well, I noticed that he had these bruises on his shoulder and upper arm, so I asked him about it."

"Okay. And?"

"And he said he was in a fight." She paused. "With you."

I looked at her. What the hell? I doubted that our fight had caused any bruising.

"He said you were just playing around and that he fell on some rocks. Is that true?"

"Well, yeah..." I began. "I mean, we did have a fight. Sort of." She held my eyes. "It was no big deal really."

She shook her head. "Boys are stupid." And then she turned back to her notebook.

Was this also part of some bro code? Some unwritten rule that told me I was supposed to back him up without knowing what he was talking about? I thought about how much pain he had seemed to be in when I jumped him, which meant he probably already had the bruises before our fight.

Maybe he had been in a fight with someone else, and didn't want Sofia to know. Or me? But who would he have had a fight with? I decided not to say anything else until I had asked Niklas about it.

I really didn't feel like being some sort of middleman between Sofia and Niklas. When we were done studying, Sofia walked me out. "Hey, I've been thinking," I said as I put my coat on.

"Okay?"

"I don't think I need a tutor any more."

"What?"

"I mean, I'm thankful for all your help – but I think I got it from here."

"Okay, sure." She shrugged. "I mean, if that's what you want."

She seemed a bit upset, but I didn't understand why. It wasn't like she was really tutoring me any more anyway. Most of the time we just did our homework together.

"Okay. I guess I'll see you later then?"

"I guess so." She smiled.

On my way out, I texted Niklas and asked him to meet me in the playground nearby.

As I was waiting for Niklas, I noticed a shoe left behind on one of the benches and decided to take a picture of it. The thought of someone accidentally leaving a shoe behind was so bizarre, but for some reason I thought it looked sort of poetic in the dusk. I uploaded the picture to Instagram and put my phone away.

A while ago, on an evening walk with Frank, I came across a building site just as the sun was about to set, and decided to try and recapture my dad's old picture of the crane.

I didn't post it on Instagram because I guess most people are not really interested in pictures of construction cranes. Personally I was quite happy with the result though. It was kind of weird and cool at the same time.

Niklas sped across the playground on his BMX. When he was closer, he slammed on the brakes, threw the bike on the ground and sat down on the bench next to me.

"What's up?" he said.

There was no way of asking him about this without revealing what Sofia had told me.

"I was just talking to Sofia," I began.

"Yeah?"

"Why did you tell her that I injured you? In our Halloween fight?"

Niklas looked at his shoes. "She asked you about that, huh?"

"Yeah."

"What did you tell her?"

"Nothing, I just confirmed that we did have a fight. But you didn't fall on any rocks that night."

"No, I know."

"So what happened?"

He stared out into the air, and I was beginning to think he wasn't going to answer me. "I fell on the ramp," he eventually said. "It collapsed when I was using it and I took a pretty hard fall. I landed on top of my bike and got the handlebar right into my side."

"Okay, so why didn't you just tell Sofia that? Why did you drag me into it?"

"I don't know." He shrugged. "I guess I thought getting hurt in a fight would sound cooler. I know that's dumb."

"It is pretty dumb," I agreed. "I mean, have you met Sofia?" There was no way she would think us fighting was cool.

"Yeah." He nodded. "She wasn't impressed. But I told her the whole thing was just a joke, anyway."

We sat in silence for a while until Niklas said that he had to go and meet Sofia. We parted ways, and I walked my bike home as the last few hours had covered the ground in frost.

I had a bad feeling that something wasn't quite right with Niklas's explanation. I tried to remember when the ramp had been broken. It felt like at least a couple of weeks before Halloween. If that was the case, there was no way the bruises would still be fresh. I felt pretty confident there was something he wasn't telling me, but I couldn't know for sure.

I put my bike in the garage. It was mid-November and it was only getting colder. The chances of frost and maybe even snow in the mornings would only increase from now on. I bent down and let the air out of the back tyre. I couldn't cycle to school with a flat tyre.

When I checked my phone, my picture of the shoe had gotten twenty-one likes. Sofia had posted a picture of her and Niklas. He had his arm around her, and standing next to him she barely reached his shoulder, which made him look even taller than he was. It already had seventy-three likes.

Johannes was making a really big deal about the science project. He had decided that at the end of the term we'd have a science fair where everyone presented their work.

I had decided to go ahead with the pinhole camera as my project. I wanted to make one anyway, and I could easily get a six on this. It was exactly the kind of thing science teachers liked (Johannes would be all over it), and it was simple to do (I already knew how to make a working one). The only challenge would be to get a good picture, which would have to be part of my presentation for me to get a full score.

The best part about my project was that I'd probably end up doing it alone. No way would anyone else be interested. The reason I was happy to do it alone was that otherwise I'd most likely get stuck with one of two types of partners:

1) Some slacker who was just trying to get in on the ride without doing any work.

2) Some overachiever who'd take over the entire project and want everything their way.

Most of the time I would be fine with the second option, but this was something I actually cared about and I wanted to do my way.

I stopped by Johannes's office after my last class, to tell him about it. And as I had expected he got really excited.

"That is a brilliant idea, Sander. It's just perfect for this project!"

I smiled.

"But you know, most kids have chosen projects already. I'd understand if you'd rather sign up for another one, to ensure that you'll have a partner."

"No, that's okay – I want to do this one."

"If you want, I could talk to someone who's chosen a less, let's say, promising project and see if they want to switch to yours."

"No, thanks. It's fine. I'm actually happy to do it on my own."

"Are you sure?"

"I'm sure."

"All right, well I am really looking forward to seeing what you'll come up with. Good luck!"

"Thanks."

I felt really good walking out of his office. Not only did he like my project, but I had a real chance of getting a six, for once. And on my own too.

I was pretty eager to get started on the project and I decided to try and take some pictures straight after school, while it was still bright outside.

I had told the others that my bike had a flat tyre and that I would have to walk to school and back until I got it fixed. After school Adrian and Filip cycled ahead as they had band and football practice to get to, but Niklas decided to walk with me.

"What do you want to do today?" he said.

"I kind of have a school project I should get started on."

"Okay. What's the project? Maybe I could help."

"I'm making a camera out of a shoebox."

"What?"

I quickly explained how it works.

"That sounds cool," Niklas said. "I want to make one too."

"You do?"

He shrugged, "Sure, why not? What else am I doing?"

"Okay. I've already started on my camera, but I think we have some materials lying around you could use for yours."

When we reached my house I quickly ran inside and found a shoebox, some black tape and an aluminium can for Niklas. I went back outside and asked him to open the door to the garage as my hands were full.

"Sure, what's the code?"

I nodded towards the wall lantern. "There should be an opener on top of that light."

He reached up and felt around with his hand until he found it. He didn't even have to stand on tiptoes. "Isn't it a bit risky to leave the opener to your garage like this?"

I shrugged. "It's a garage. What would anyone steal?"

He pressed the button and put the opener back in its place. "I don't know, your car?"

"Well, we don't leave the key to the car lying around." I walked into the garage and dumped everything on the workbench. "Are you ready to get started?"

"Sure."

Niklas started painting his box, while I finished making my camera. I had to go inside for a minute so I could load the camera in darkness and when I came back Niklas had finished painting.

"What do I do with it, now?" he said.

"It needs to be completely dry before you can continue. And if you don't mind, I kind of wanted to start taking pictures as soon as possible."

"Okay, I guess I'll finish it later. What are you taking a picture of?"

"Actually, I've been wanting to take a picture of the vine on your porch."

"You want to go to my place?"

"If you don't mind, yeah."

He frowned. "To take a picture of a vine?"

I laughed. "I know, it sounds dumb. But I think it will work for this project."

"Okay…" He shrugged. "My vine is at your service."

By the time we reached Niklas's house, the sun had disappeared behind some clouds and it wasn't long before we would lose daylight.

I also realized that I had forgotten to bring any extra photo paper, so I only had one shot.

"Can you take pictures inside instead?" Niklas suggested.

"I can try. I'll need a lamp, though."

We went inside and walked into the kitchen. Niklas stopped by the fridge. "Do you want a beer?"

I shook my head. "No, thanks, I'm good."

He opened a bottle and took a sip. "I thought all artists liked to get inspired by the help of a little booze. To get the creative juices flowing."

I thought about my last experience with alcohol. I felt

a lot of things that night, but creative definitely wasn't one of them. "I'll take my chances," I said.

"All right, suit yourself."

We went into the next room, and I realized I hadn't been beyond the kitchen before. I looked around for something to take a picture of, but I wasn't feeling inspired. I walked past a dining table and continued to the main part of the living room which consisted of a lot of black furniture. The leather couch, TV unit and table were all black, along with a chest of drawers placed under a giant mirror. There were all kinds of knick-knacks everywhere, like candlesticks and lanterns and a few wall stickers that said things like "family" and "love".

Niklas took a sip of his beer. "You got any ideas?"

I pointed at the dining table. "I guess I could place the camera here and set up a lamp behind it."

He pointed at the giant mirror. "Won't you catch your own reflection?"

"Yeah, that's kind of the idea." I shrugged. "Well, the camera at least. I'll step out of the way. I don't think the camera will be able to capture me unless I stand still."

"Okay, you're the artist."

Niklas fetched a desk lamp and set it up on one end of the table, while I placed the camera on the other end.

We heard the sound of the front door opening, and

Niklas hurried to hide his beer behind a plant. Maybe his stepdad wasn't too pleased with him drinking beer after all.

Soon a male voice shouted from the kitchen, "Niklas! Get in here."

"You have everything you need?" Niklas asked me.

I nodded.

"Niklas! Kitchen," the voice shouted, louder this time.

"I'll be right back," Niklas said, and he left the room.

I removed the black tape from the camera and set the timer on my phone for two minutes. I could hear the conversation from the kitchen.

"Do you have something to tell me?" the man's voice said. He spoke in a low, but stern tone.

"No," Niklas replied.

"You want to explain where my beer is?"

"I don't know."

"I suppose it just walked out of my fridge on its own?"

I felt awkward, standing there listening to something I wasn't supposed to listen to, and I couldn't leave because I would have to go through the kitchen to get out. I tried to focus on what I was doing. I kept my eyes on my phone and watched the timer count down.

"I didn't touch it," Niklas said, raising his voice.

"Don't you walk away from me!" the man shouted.

The alarm sounded on my phone and the voices in the kitchen fell silent behind me as I covered the pinhole with the tape.

"Hi there." It was Niklas's stepdad, speaking in a much lower and gentler tone now. I turned around. Niklas was standing in the kitchen doorway next to a tall, slim man with a neatly trimmed beard and a nice shirt.

"Hi," I said.

"I didn't realize we had company." The man smiled.

"Oh well, it's just me." I didn't really know what to say. "Sander."

"Nice to meet you, Sander. I'm afraid we have to cut the visit short today. Niklas has some chores he needs to do. Homework and such."

"Yeah, that's cool."

I grabbed my camera and Niklas walked me out. The man smiled at me again as we walked past him to get to the front door. I could still feel the tension hanging in the room, and I really didn't mind leaving. I figured maybe Niklas wanted to leave for a bit too. "You could do your homework at my place if you wanted," I suggested. "And have dinner with us. If you want, I mean."

"Thanks," Niklas said. "Another time."

When I got home I went out to the garage to tidy up the mess I had made, and threw away all the leftover pieces of paper and other bits I didn't need any more. That's when I saw something on the floor.

A key.

It was the key to the gun cabinet. I was sure I had checked everywhere on the floor for that key, but I guess I hadn't. Me panicking and running over to Niklas's house could have all been avoided, if I had just checked properly. I decided to put it back straight away to avoid something similar happening in the future. I got the stepladder and put the key back in its place.

I was sitting in the school library, reading a book called *Secrets of the Darkroom*. It was the first day of preparation for the science project and I'd decided to do some research. I would have to document the science behind the entire process in a report.

"Hey, partner."

I looked up as Sofia sat down at my table.

"What?"

"I'm joining your science project. Unless that whole 'I-don't-need-a-tutor-any-more' was just your way of telling me to get out of your face?"

"Of course not."

"Great."

"But I thought everyone had chosen projects already?"

"My partner fell through. She's home with pneumonia. Very selfish, I know."

I stared at her, trying to take in what she was telling me.

"That was a joke, Sander."

I tried to smile.

"Anyway," she continued, "I talked to Johannes and he advised me to pick another project, since the one I'd chosen is way too big to do on my own. And then Veronica can do a make-up project once she's back."

"Who?"

"My previous partner."

"Right."

"Your project was the only one left that seemed interesting, so here I am."

I nodded. Of course she would think this was interesting. And it was one of the projects that had the highest chance of getting top marks if done correctly. Of course she would choose this.

"We should get started right away. We have a lot to do. I know nothing about pinhole cameras. Do you?"

"A little."

She took her phone out and typed in as she read out loud, "How to make a pinhole camera."

I picked up my pencil and started chewing on it.

"All these things should be easy to get a hold of," she said. "Do you want to go shopping together? Or do you want me to get them and you can just pay me back?"

"Actually, I've already made the camera," I whispered. "We could just use the one I have."

"Oh, that was fast. Well, let me know how much you spent and I can reimburse you."

I shook my head. "Not necessary. I mean, I pretty much had everything at the house already."

"Okay, great." She took up her phone again. "How are we going to develop the picture?"

"What?"

"In your description of the project it said that you are going to present a developed photo. Don't we need a darkroom for that?"

"I…umm. I guess I hadn't thought of that." I couldn't take her to Vemund's place.

She looked at me like I was an idiot. "Well, we need to figure that out as soon as possible. We can't leave it to the last minute."

After school I stopped by Vemund's house. I'd reached the end of the film in my Olympus, and I was hoping he could help me develop it.

I rang his doorbell and while I was waiting for him to open the door, I couldn't help but look over my shoulder to see if anyone I knew was nearby. I still didn't want anyone to see me going to his house because, if you think about it, it is a bit weird for a fifteen-year-old to hang out at an old man's house. Especially the guy who is known for being the town crazy.

The door opened and Vemund's face broke into a huge smile.

"Sander! To what do I owe this honour?"

I held up my camera. "I could use your help, if you don't mind."

"Of course." He opened the door all the way so I could go in. "You know, you don't have to ring the doorbell every time you want to visit. If the door is unlocked it means that I'm home and you are welcome."

"Okay, sure," I said and felt relieved at the thought of not having to stand and wait on his doorstep any more.

"I trust you," he continued. "We are friends now."

We went down to the basement, and Vemund took my camera.

"Did you rewind the film?"

I nodded and he opened the camera and removed the canister holding the film. He pulled out a pair of reading glasses from his breast pocket and put them on his nose so he could study the film closer.

"Thirty-five millimetres?" he said.

"Yeah."

He turned off the lights and switched the safelight on. Then he opened the canister with something that looked like a bottle opener and took the film out. He gave the film back to me. "Hold this for me, will you?"

He started searching through drawers and boxes until he found what he was looking for. He held up a spool the size of his fist. "This is a film reel." He loaded the film onto the reel and then he placed it inside a cylindrical container.

"And this is the developing tank," he said and filled the container with chemicals. "It's a whole little darkroom of its own." He put the lid on the container, switched the lights back on and set the timer. He turned the tank upside down, up and down, over and over again. "So your pictures don't come out streaky," he explained.

The thought of my photos being in the tank filled with chemicals was a bit scary, as there is a chance you can ruin the whole film if you don't know what you're doing. But I knew I could trust Vemund with it.

The timer rang and Vemund poured out the first set of developer chemicals and added the stop bath to the tank. He tipped this up and down too.

"If you wanted to make a darkroom at home," I asked him, "just to develop pinhole photos…would any room do?"

"As long as you are able to make it completely dark, yes."

"What about the chemicals? Are they easy to get hold of?"

"I used to buy them at the photo shop in town. I don't know if they still have them."

I figured it might be easier to get them online. I would have to order them soon to make sure they arrived in time.

"Are they expensive?"

"I'm not sure. It's been a long time since I bought any. Why?"

"I was just wondering."

The timer rang again, and this time Vemund emptied out the stop bath and added the fixer. He turned the tank upside down and back again, then left it.

"You know you can use my darkroom whenever you want. For as long as you want."

"Yeah, I know. Thanks."

He frowned. "Something wrong?"

I shook my head. "Nope, everything is fine."

"Are you sure?"

"Yeah." I pointed at a stack of photos. "Did you take these?"

"A long time ago."

I started flipping through them. They were taken in the town centre and they had to be old, because most of the shops in the photos had been closed down and replaced by others by now. The light and composition was perfect in every single picture.

After a few minutes the timer rang. Vemund emptied the tank. Then he filled the container with cold water from a jug he had prepped on the side. It had a thermometer in it and he checked the temperature of the water before filling the container. He inverted the tank a few times, emptied it, refilled it, emptied it and refilled it again. After that, he took the film off the reel and I helped him unroll it, before we clipped it to the clothes line to remove any excess water.

"It needs to dry for at least a few hours before we can cut it up," Vemund said. "Do you want some coffee while we wait?"

I wanted to accept because I liked the idea of him thinking I drank coffee, which I don't. But I couldn't really stay there for hours without my family wondering where I was. "Actually, I have to go," I said. "I'll stop by some other time though."

"Sure, any time. Next we'll turn the negatives into photos."

"Great," I said. "Thanks."

When I got home, Frank greeted me at the door as usual. Jakob also sort of greeted me, by smacking me over my head on his way out. It might sound weird, but when he does things like that I sort of feel like he acknowledges me as a brother. He may only fight Adrian, but he smacks both of us over the head.

That night I took my injection before bed like I always do. I couldn't remember how long it had been since I'd grown. A month and a half? More? I wasn't sure. I threw the used needle in the sharps disposal container and went up to my room.

I got the measurement tape from my drawer, lined up against the door frame and made a mark above my head with a pencil. The mark was in the exact same spot.

According to my phone, my appointment at the hospital was under a month away. They would never renew my growth hormone prescription if I didn't start growing soon. I had to do something.

28

Sofia and I were sitting in my kitchen doing more research. I was meant to be looking for an answer to our whole development issue, but my mind kept wandering. I kept Googling things like *growth hormone treatment not working any more*, which led me to a bunch of useless articles, like "Twelve Ways to Increase Human Growth Hormone Levels Naturally". All the articles had the same sort of tips. *Decrease your sugar intake. Don't eat too much right before bed.*

But I was way past these kinds of natural remedies. What I needed was a miracle.

I opened a new tab and tried to find out if it was possible to buy the photo-developing chemicals online. There were several international online shops selling them, but then we would have to pay for shipping and they would probably not even get here in time. I found a local shop, but it was expensive. Each bottle was over two hundred kroner. I didn't really have that kind of money. We would also need suitable trays, tongs and a red light bulb.

I looked at Sofia. Why did she have to get involved? If it wasn't for her, I could have just developed the photo at Vemund's, like I had planned.

"Maybe we can do the project without having a photo developed?" I said. "We can still document the process."

She looked up from her phone. "Actually, I think I found a way to solve it."

"You did?"

"I found this site showing how you can make your own developing solution using household items."

"How?"

"All you need is water, lemon juice, vitamin C tablets, coffee and bicarbonate of soda."

I frowned and she handed me her phone so I could see for myself. The page showed instructions of how to make a developing solution and a stop bath with the ingredients Sofia had listed.

"What about the fixer?"

"What's a fixer?"

"The fixer stabilizes the image. Makes it all come together."

"Well, according to this it doesn't look like we need it."

"But this only gives us a negative. There's a different process to turn it into a positive image."

"Is it hard?"

"I think we need a photo enlarger."

"Okay, let's check. Maybe there's an alternative way to do it." She turned back to her phone and I turned back to my laptop. I typed in *Human Growth Hormone Alternative Methods* and I found an article called "A Safer, Cheaper Way to Increase Human Growth Hormone Levels".

> *These days we have numerous growth hormone peptides and growth hormone-releasing hormones that can boost your growth hormone levels.*
>
> *The combination of peptides and growth hormone releasers can increase your growth hormone production.*

I read through the entire article. My doctors had never mentioned any alternative methods, but that was probably because up until now the methods they had prescribed had been working. This seemed like it could be the answer to everything. I needed to see a doctor. And fast.

"What are we going to take a picture of, anyway?" Sofia said.

"I don't know. We could try different things."

"What about a picture of a meal?"

"What?" Was she being serious?

"Or something else that is trending on Instagram, like fitness. We could put a humorous spin on it. 'This is how much work it would be to document your fitness programme without a digital camera' kind of thing."

I looked at her. I hated the idea. "I don't want to take a picture of Instagram trends."

"Okay, what's your idea?"

"I don't know. We need a lot of light, so we should take a picture outside."

"So, like a sunset?"

"There is not a lot of light during a sunset."

"Okay, well, whatever you want to do. As long as it is something that catches people's attention. We probably shouldn't just take a picture of a tree, or you know, a bench."

I looked up. A bench? Like the one on my Instagram account? "The point is to show that you can take a good picture using a box and some black tape," I muttered. "Not something we can put a hashtag on."

She became busy on her phone again and we both went quiet.

"Hey, I think I found something," she said after a while. "Seems like it's possible to solve the whole 'negative-to-positive-thing' digitally."

"Digitally?"

"Yeah, I'm not sure I understand it though. Let me send you the link."

I looked at the link she sent me and started reading through the different steps.

"Seems like they scan in the pinhole negatives and then they upload it to some photo editing software to invert the colours?" Sofia said.

I nodded. "This actually looks really simple. I guess we could try that."

"Great. That will save us a lot of time, and we can document how we mixed old methods with modern technology."

"Yeah." To me it seemed more fun to do everything the old-fashioned way and keep it authentic, but at the moment I didn't really care. It wasn't my project any more. Sofia had taken over and I didn't feel like spending more time on it than I had to.

"Did you say you already have the camera?"

"Yeah, it's in the garage. I made it before I knew you were joining. We just need the ingredients for the developing solution and a red light bulb, and we're good to go."

"Okay, that's brilliant." She started putting her things in her backpack. "I actually need to get going, but we can meet up in a couple of days?"

"Sure."

"Great, I can pick up all the stuff we need on my way over." She shouldered her backpack and gave me a quick wave as she left.

I turned back to my laptop. I wondered if it was possible to book an appointment with a general physician without my mum knowing. I'd rather leave her out of it if I could. I knew she would tell me to wait and see what they said at my next check-up at the hospital first. She'd say that not growing was not the end of the world. That the most important thing was I was healthy and happy. But how could I be happy without growing?

According to Google, the Norwegian law said that kids between twelve and sixteen could book a doctor's appointment without their parents knowing about it. Parents had access to their children's records until aged sixteen, but between twelve and sixteen, details could be kept confidential at the patient's request, unless it was concerning something serious like surgery or cancer.

A change in my treatment plan was probably something that my mum would need to agree to. But I could still talk to a doctor on my own and suggest the alternative treatment. If the doctor said it worked, I was sure my mum would let me do it.

29

The next day the hours at school seemed to go by even slower than usual. I'd booked a doctor's appointment for three o'clock and I was actually kind of excited to get there. It was clear that my current treatment wasn't working and maybe this was the answer. Or maybe the doctor would have a different suggestion.

I made my way over to the health centre right after school. I had told the others they could just cycle ahead as I still hadn't gotten around to fixing my bike. It had been a long time since I had been to the local doctor's, because I always had my check-ups at the hospital. The waiting room was full of plants. They were so green they made all the patients in the room look pale. I wanted to take a picture but was afraid someone would catch me doing it.

I didn't have to wait long until I got called in. As I walked into the treatment room, an older man called

Dr Greger greeted me and told me to have a seat. He said that my regular doctor was on leave and that he was filling in for him. I didn't really know my regular doctor too well so I didn't mind. He sat down in his chair and put on the glasses he had hanging on a cord around his neck. Then he started typing on his keyboard. "Let me just pull up your file," he said. He peered over his glasses. "SRS?"

I nodded.

"That's a very rare condition."

Wow, nothing gets past this guy. I didn't say anything. I just nodded again.

He took off his glasses and leaned back in his chair. "All right," he said. "What can I do for you today?"

"Well, my growth hormone treatment is not really working any more. I mean, I haven't been growing lately. Not in a while actually."

"Mm-hmm." Dr Greger squinted and waited for me to continue.

"So I was wondering if there might be an alternative treatment."

He glanced at the computer screen. "You are fifteen?"

I nodded.

"You know, children start on growth hormones at different ages for various reasons and will stay on them until they finish puberty. Once you finish puberty, the hormones will no longer have any effect."

I really wished this old guy would stop saying puberty. "Yeah, I know, but I found this." I took out my phone and pulled up the article from the other day. "There might be another way."

I handed him the phone and he took it. He put his glasses back on and started scrolling, with an uninterested look on his face. He was scrolling too fast to be able to read what it actually said.

He handed me my phone back and leaned forward in his chair. "Do you have a check-up scheduled at the hospital?"

"Yeah. In December."

"Okay, so I suggest you wait until then. They'll take a blood test and they will be able tell if the growth hormones are still having an effect."

"But I already know they don't have an effect any more. By then it might be too late!"

He gave me an apologetic smile. "Even if I thought there was an alternative method, I can't change your treatment plan. You would have to discuss it with your specialist."

I clenched my fists. I could feel tears pricking behind my eyes. It was clear that he wasn't interested in listening to me. He hadn't even looked at the article properly.

"They won't renew my prescription." I swallowed. "Not if it's not working."

The doctor nodded. "You are probably right about that. You know, you could still grow a few more centimetres."

"Or not," I mumbled.

"Either way you won't find the answers you're looking for on the internet, I'm afraid. There are tons of websites promoting alternative treatments for increasing your growth, but they don't have any proven effects. People behind these websites are just trying to earn money."

I didn't say anything. I just kept clenching and unclenching my fists.

Dr Greger shrugged. "You have to trust your specialist. They know which treatment is right for you."

When I got back home I went straight to my room, completely ignoring Frank's joyful greeting. I found a pencil and stood next to the door. After I'd marked the door frame I turned around and looked at it. I was 153 centimetres. The numbers hadn't moved. They were standing still.

I would never grow taller than 153 centimetres.

I threw the pencil across the room, but it wasn't very satisfying. I needed to throw something harder. I picked up a Rubik's cube from my bookshelf and threw it the same way I'd thrown the pencil. It hit the wall before dropping and knocking over my desk lamp.

I ran back downstairs and continued down to the basement where my brothers were in the middle of a fight. Jakob was sitting on Adrian's chest, trying to prise the remote control out of his hands.

"I was here first," Adrian yelled.

"Where? On the Earth? Pretty sure you weren't," Jakob said.

"Get off me!"

"Just give me the remote now and I don't have to hurt you!"

"Fine, take it!"

Jakob let go of his grip and held out his hand for Adrian to give it to him. Instead Adrian knocked Jakob over the forehead with it.

Jakob lifted his hand to his head. "Oh, that's it, you're dead!"

And that is when I jumped on Jakob's back.

Jakob let out a muffled "What the hell" under my arm, which I held in a tight grip around his neck. He put both of his hands on my arm, trying to get me to loosen my grip, and Adrian used this opportunity to get up from the floor. Then Jakob held on to my arm so tight that I actually couldn't let go.

Adrian picked up the remote and hit him on the head with it again, which made him let go of my arm, and both of us ran upstairs.

"You guys are dead," Jakob yelled after us.

We ran all the way up to my room, and I locked the door just in case he decided to come after us.

After we had caught our breath we looked at each other and burst out laughing. We sat down on my bed, and I started an episode of *Rick and Morty* on my laptop. A few minutes later there was a scratching sound at the door. That would be Frank. I got up to let him in.

"Don't open it," Adrian said. "It's probably Jakob pretending to be the dog."

"He is not that smart," I laughed. I opened the door, and Frank ran into my room wagging his tail. I bent down and gave him a good cuddle. I felt so bad for ignoring him earlier that I decided to let him sleep in my room that night.

"We should team up against Jakob more often," Adrian said. "We totally beat him!"

I shrugged. "Yet he is the one watching TV in the basement right now."

I managed to convince Sofia that the subject of our photo needed to be as simple as possible. I explained that it was better to have a simple theme, with great execution than to take a complicated idea and just get an average result. When I put it that way she agreed.

"Besides, nature photos are also popular on Instagram," she said.

"Thank God," I said.

She laughed. "And for the presentation we could put #nofilter under the photo."

"Fine," I said. I still hated her idea to put an Instagram spin on it, but I didn't want to keep arguing about it.

The storage room in my basement was going to be our darkroom. It didn't have a window, so when the lights were off it became completely dark. We'd carried in the ingredients for the solution, together with measuring cups, coffee filters, two trays and a couple of tongs I'd taken from the kitchen. I had also brought my desk lamp and put a red bulb in it for us to use as a safelight.

We decided to make the solutions first, as they needed to sit for a while before they were ready to use. Sofia pulled out her phone to check the instructions. She mixed the ingredients for the development solution and poured it into the first tray, and I made the stopper solution and poured it into the second tray.

"We need to use the safelight every time we load and unload the film," I explained. I turned off the main light and switched on the lamp, leaving the room in a dim red light.

When I opened the camera, Sofia said, "There's already photo paper in it."

I had forgotten about the picture I had taken at Niklas's house. "Oh there's already something on that," I said. I removed it and put it in a shoebox I found on one of the shelves. That would serve as a safe place for the negatives until I developed them. After I had put in a new piece of photo paper, Sofia picked up the box.

"So where should we go? If we had someone who could drive us, we could go out to the beach."

"It's better if we stay close to the house. We need to reload the camera in the darkroom between every picture."

"Oh right, I didn't think of that."

"And we should probably take a few, to make sure we get a good one."

"So where are we going?"

"To the backyard."

"And what are we taking a picture of? Just, like a tree?"

"Exactly," I said. "Or a bench."

We decided to go for a birch tree in the backyard as our subject. We carried the table down from the terrace and placed it in the garden so that we could rest the camera on it. I placed it in position, set the timer on my phone for three minutes and removed the tape. And we waited.

"We should probably try a few different exposure times," I said.

Sofia nodded. "We just need to write down the correct time for each photo. So we can put it in the report."

"Good idea," I said, and for the first time I was glad Sofia was on the project with me. She really did think of everything.

The alarm went off, and I covered the hole with the piece of tape. "Now we need to go to the darkroom and load it with a new photo," I said. We repeated this four times and it was a pretty tedious process. Sometimes it's the result that makes a project exciting.

When we came back to the basement for the fourth

time, the boys were spread out on the couch playing video games. Sofia put her arm on Niklas's shoulder and squeezed it gently. "Hi," she said.

"Hi." He gave her a quick smile before returning to his game.

"What have you guys been doing?" Adrian asked.

"We've been in the yard taking pictures of a tree," Sofia said. "Now we're going to develop the photos."

Filip paused the game. "If we do the science fair thing next year, I am going to make my own silver bullets, just like the ones in *Teen Wolf*. And engrave them with my initials."

"You have to have a functioning experiment," I said. "So you need to prove that what you make actually works."

"I could set up target practice in the gymnasium. And use your dad's hunting rifle as my weapon."

"Yeah, I'm sure they'd let you do that," Adrian laughed.

"Even if they did, you'd never be able to make functioning bullets," Niklas said.

"It's just too bad we don't have the key to the gun cabinet any more." Filip shrugged. "Now we'll never know."

"Actually, I found the key," I said. "That's not the part of this plan that's at fault."

"All right," Sofia said, looking at me. "Shall we continue?"

I nodded, and we went into the storage room. I switched the lights off and turned the red light on, and we sat down on the floor.

Sofia picked up one of the pieces of photo paper. "So do I just drop it in?"

I nodded and she gently slipped it into the solution.

And then all we could do was wait. We sat there in complete silence, and suddenly I became really aware of how weird this was. I was sitting on the floor of a closet-sized room with a girl. In the dark. Just me and a girl. And her boyfriend was in the next room.

Sofia used the tongs to flip the photo. Did she find this weird? It didn't seem like she did. She seemed all cool and chilled. "Do I move it to the next tray yet?"

The details in the photo still looked really vague. "Not yet," I said, and for some reason my voice came out really hoarse. I cleared my throat and said, "I'd leave it for a bit longer."

Sofia was paying close attention to what was happening to the photo. "Wow," she said. "You can totally see the tree. This is so cool!"

"Yeah." I smiled. "You should move it now."

She picked it up with the tongs and dropped it in the second tray.

"You need to use the other tongs now," I said. "So we

don't mix the chemicals." She dropped the first tongs in the first tray and picked up the second pair.

I liked teaching Sofia the things Vemund had taught me. And even if it was completely weird to sit in this darkroom with a girl, it was also kind of nice.

After a couple of minutes she lifted the photo from the stop bath and let the solution drip from it, back into the tray.

"What do I do with it now?"

"Oh, shoot." I'd completely forgotten that we needed to dry it off. As we hadn't used a fixer, it didn't need rinsing so the drying part shouldn't take as long. I pulled the trays apart and leaned the negative on the edge of each tray, letting the solution drip down on the floor between them. I could already tell that it wouldn't be as sharp as if we'd used real chemicals.

"Perfect," Sofia said. "So, what exactly is the next step? You scan the negatives into the computer and work some sort of magic on them to turn them into positive photos?"

"Yeah. It's actually a really simple step. The computer pretty much does the work for you."

Sofia raised her eyebrows. "Sounds like proper MacGyver magic to me."

"MacGyver?"

She nodded. "And not the poorly imitated version that's

on TV these days. You are obviously the original one."

I had no idea what she was talking about. "Who is MacGyver?"

"Oh my God." She shook her head laughing. "Your lack of pop culture knowledge is shocking."

"So are you going to tell me who he is?"

"No. Look it up." Sofia picked up the next photo from the floor. "Do you want to do this one?"

I shrugged. "You can keep going, if you want."

When we were done, Sofia said, "I guess that's it," and got up from the floor.

"Yup." I got up too, and switched the main light back on.

"So, you'll invert the negatives and print them out?"

I nodded. "I'll turn the negatives into positives."

She laughed. "You should get that on a cushion."

We walked back into the furnished part of the basement.

"I'm leaving now," she told Niklas. "Are you coming too?"

He nodded and got up from his chair. "I'm trusting you with these photos, MacGyver," Sofia said, as she walked up the staircase with Niklas. "Take good care of them."

Apparently MacGyver was this guy from a TV show in the 90s who could fix anything and everything with a piece of duct tape and a penknife. There was also a new show starring the same character, but according to hardcore fans he just couldn't live up to the original.

I smiled. I was the original.

I closed the browser and started scanning in all the negatives Sofia and I had taken. They looked awful. Well, that wasn't entirely true. Some of the pictures themselves would have been all right – it was the development process that made them look awful. A small part of me still hoped they would look okay once I inverted the colours.

They didn't.

I had to find a way to fix it. I was MacGyver, after all.

The day after, I brought the camera out to the backyard and tried to retake the same photos we had taken of the birch tree earlier. There was even better light that day, increasing the chances of taking decent photos. Afterwards I put all the negatives in the shoebox to keep them from being ruined by the light.

At dinner I noticed that Jakob had a bump on his forehead, from where Adrian had hit him with the remote, and for some reason this made me laugh. It just made him look so silly. Like a cartoon character.

As he hadn't retaliated by now he probably wasn't going to. He has a bit of an explosive temper, but he never stays mad for long. My dad was like that too. At least that is what Mum always says. When Jakob blows up she'll sigh and go, "Oh, you are just like your dad."

But I don't remember my dad being angry. I only remember him being the kindest and greatest dad ever. A guy who would lift me up in his big arms like I weighed nothing at all. (Which I sort of did.) Who would tell me that I was the toughest guy he knew, even though that clearly wasn't true, and who would listen to me talk about all the *Avatar* characters in detail for ages, even though he had no interest in them at all.

Sometimes I forget what he looked like. Of course, I have a general idea – dark hair, broad shoulders, strong chin – but sometimes his facial features, especially around the eyes and nose, vanish a bit for me. And then if I look at a picture of him, I remember him properly again.

Mum also tells Adrian that he is just like my dad from time to time. Adrian has this cheeky smile that he does sometimes when he wants something or knows he's in trouble. Apparently my dad used to do the same thing and my mum could never stay mad at him for long. Adrian could get away with murder with that smile.

I would love to have inherited a trait like that from my dad, even if it was something unflattering like a bad habit or a hot temper. But Mum has never said, *"Oh you are just like your dad,"* to me.

"Do you want the last piece of chicken?" Mum asked Jakob, shoving the plate closer to him. He shook his head. "I'm good. Maybe Sander wants it."

Adrian and I quickly exchanged looks, because there really wasn't any reason why he would mention me over him. I was pretty full, but I ate the chicken anyway. Protein makes you strong. Or so they say.

32

The next day I took the shoebox full of pinhole negatives over to Vemund's house so I could develop them in time for the science fair. I walked into his house without ringing the doorbell and found him sitting in his armchair listening to the radio. As always, he was happy to see me.

"Sander!" he said, and he turned the radio off. "I feel like I haven't seen you in quite some time. I thought you might have forgotten about your negatives in my basement?"

"Never," I said. "I knew they would be safe here."

"So are you ready to continue?"

"I'd love to." I held up the shoebox. "But first I need to develop these for school. Maybe you'd like to help?"

In the basement, the roll of negatives from my Olympus camera was still hanging on the clothes line, and Vemund unclipped it and put it away to make room for the new images. I lined up three trays and filled them with the different chemicals. Vemund turned off all the lights and I turned on the safelight.

I opened the shoebox, and Vemund peeked inside.

"You've been keeping these out of the light?" he asked.

I nodded. "I've used a safelight every time I loaded and unloaded the camera."

"Just like a pro."

"I learned from the best." I smiled.

I dropped one of the negatives into the first tray. After a few seconds I could see edges of the photo sheet getting darker and the image started to become visible. Once it was finished, I took it out and Vemund hung it on the clothes line, where an inverted image of the birch tree in my yard was now fully visible.

"It looks good," Vemund said.

"Thanks."

We continued developing the rest of the negatives. I only needed one for the presentation and I wanted the best one. They all pretty much looked the same, even if the exposure time had been slightly different.

"My dad also liked photography," I said.

"He did?"

I nodded. "He never mentioned it to you?"

"No, I didn't know him too well. He was always friendly and said hello whenever I saw him, but we didn't really talk too often."

"Mum said they came over for a cupcakes and jazz night once."

He laughed. "That may be. I don't remember that particular night, but my wife did like theme nights. Had I known your dad was into photography I would have invited him over to check out my darkroom." He paused, then added, "I'm sure he would have loved to share this with you."

I nodded. I wondered if I would have been into photography if my dad hadn't died. Finding the camera with the film made me interested because it was like discovering an unknown, hidden piece of him. But if he had suggested we'd go out to take photos together, would I have been interested? Or would I have turned him down, the way I did with fishing? I would never know for sure, but I hoped I would have been interested.

"Is that it?" Vemund said, hanging the fifth image of the birch tree on the clothes line.

"One more," I said and dropped the last negative into the tray.

"That might be the perfect one," Vemund said.

"Exactly."

As the details started forming. I noticed it wasn't a picture of a birch tree. It was the picture I had taken at Niklas's place.

"What's this?" Vemund said.

"Oh, this is something I took a while ago. I'm not using this for the project."

"You took a picture of the camera," Vemund said. "That's clever."

"Thanks."

I used the tong to flip the negative over. I didn't really know why, but I had seen Vemund do it. More and more details started forming and it became clear that it wasn't a very good picture. There was too much clutter in the background. Candlesticks and knick-knacks.

Soon two people started becoming visible in the background. A man with a neatly trimmed beard and a boy with a Mohawk. I kept flipping the picture back and forth to check if it was ready.

As the background details started coming together, the man and the boy became fully visible. And that's when I realized something was very, very wrong.

I looked at Vemund. He saw it too. Or maybe he just noticed that I looked worried. In any case his face seemed pretty serious as he took the tongs from me.

The picture showed the man grabbing the boy's arm.

And maybe this on its own didn't have to mean anything, because I guess someone can have a hold of someone's arm without it being violent. It's hard to tell from a picture. Especially a picture taken with a pinhole camera via a mirror.

But the man looked angry. His jaw was clenched and his eyes were white and shiny. Of course, the white and shiny eyes were because it was a negative, but it still freaked me out.

And I had been there that day. The man with the neat beard and nice shirt had sounded angry. And threatening. And I had left the house.

I thought about Niklas's bruises, and about what Sofia had said...

Niklas had clearly been lying about something.

I should have seen it sooner.

When I told Vemund all this, he asked who the boy was and wanted his contact details.

"What are you going to do?"

"I'm going to call social services."

"Wait. Don't you think that's a bit drastic? Shouldn't we wait?" I hated the idea of ambushing Niklas with this. I wanted to talk to him before doing anything. He should get a say in how this was handled. "I could be wrong."

Vemund shrugged. "When you call social services to

raise a concern about something like this, in the first instance they will pay the family a visit and check up on them. If everything is okay, then no harm done. It's much worse if something is going on and we don't make the call."

But everything wasn't okay, and I knew it.

I used my phone to take a picture of the negative and inverted the colours so I could see it more clearly, but it didn't change anything. It just became clearer.

I should have seen it sooner.

"What will happen to Niklas? I mean, will he go into foster care?"

"Possibly. They will probably look for a relative to take care of him. If not, foster care will be the next step."

I didn't say anything.

"A scarier thought, however," Vemund said, "is what will happen to him if we don't make the call."

I collected my things and put my coat on. And then I gave Vemund Niklas's details. Because I had to.

I left before he called them. I knew what he was doing was right, but I still felt bad about it.

As I left the house I called Niklas, but he didn't pick up. I texted him and asked if everything was okay, but he didn't reply.

Eventually I texted Niklas the picture and said: *Hey,*

I just found this picture and wanted to check in. Let me know if I can do anything.

He still didn't reply.

That night I lay awake for hours not being able to sleep. I'd brought Frank to bed and he definitely knew something was up. He put his head on my chest and just looked at me with sad eyes. When I patted his head he licked my hand, trying to make it all better. But he couldn't.

Eventually I did fall asleep. And then, what felt like five minutes later, my alarm went off.

33

It was the day of the science fair, and Sofia was completely stressed out. I didn't really understand why, because even if we didn't end up getting a six on this project she would still get five in this class, maybe even a six. She called me in the morning before school, to remind me to bring the camera and the photos. Like I would forget.

I had a lot of stuff to carry and Mum had offered to go into work a bit later than usual so she could drive me.

I put my bag, the pinhole camera and the folder with the photos in the garage, so I'd have everything ready to go after my morning walk with Frank. But when I came back from the walk our car was not in the garage.

I called Mum, and she picked up after three rings.

"Where are you?" I asked.

"I'm at work."

"You were supposed to take me to school."

"Oh – I'm so sorry, Sander, I completely forgot. I got called into a meeting and had to leave in a rush."

"Can you come back and pick me up?"

"I'm sorry, I don't have time now. The meeting is about to start."

I paused. "Okay," I said, even though it wasn't. I knew there was nothing she could do, and I didn't have time to argue.

"Sorry."

"It's okay."

"Hey, good luck on your presentation."

"Thanks," I said, and I hung up without saying bye.

Adrian had already left and I was running late. I hurried to the garage and put the photos in my backpack before shouldering it. Then I picked up the camera and rushed out the garage door as it was closing. The puddles were frozen and the streets were slippery in certain places, but I tried to hurry the best I could. Once I reached the main road I started running, as it was less icy.

Sofia had wanted us to meet early to set everything up and go over our presentation, but that wasn't going to happen now. I'd be lucky if I was even there on time. I realized I should have texted her to let her know I was running late, but I didn't want to waste time stopping now. When I jogged into the gymnasium, panting, class was about to start.

Sofia was standing by a table. She had put up pictures on the wall behind her showing how to build a pinhole camera.

"Where were you?" she hissed. "It's about to start!"

"I'm sorry."

"Why didn't you answer your phone? I've been trying to call you."

I put the camera on the table. "It was in my backpack," I said between breaths. "Sorry, I didn't have time to get it."

I looked around the room. Everyone was busy setting up, and no one seemed to be finished. We weren't doing the presentation until later in the afternoon. There was no real need to come in early.

"Do you have the photos?" Sofia asked.

I opened my backpack and handed her the folder.

Then Adrian and Filip walked in. "What are you guys doing here?" I asked. "Why are you not in class?"

"Our teacher is sick," Adrian said. "The sub said we should go check out your science fair." I noticed more and more people from their class walking in.

"Where is Niklas?" Sofia asked, as she started going through the folder in her hand.

"He's not in school today."

"Is he sick?"

"No clue."

"Weird. He seemed fine yesterday. I hope he won't miss the presentation."

Niklas not being in school made me feel nervous. I couldn't help thinking that this might have had something to do with me speaking to Vemund the day before.

Adrian shrugged. "We're going to check out the other stands." He gave a quick wave, and him and Filip moved along.

Sofia turned to me, holding up the photos. "What are these?"

They were the photos I'd taken on my own. "Oh I took some new ones."

"They are so sharp. How did you develop them?"

"I...uhm...I got hold of some chemicals."

"You used real chemicals?"

I nodded.

She quickly flipped through the folder. "Where are the photos we took?"

"They should be in there."

"They're not," she looked at me. "We need those photos."

"Can't we use the ones we have? I mean, they are better."

"Our report says we used a developer made of household supplies only."

Crap. I'd been so concerned about getting better photos I'd completely forgotten about the report.

"We can't use these."

Sofia looked really mad. I had wanted to be MacGyver, but instead I made a mess of everything. "I'll go home and get them."

She sighed. "Well, hurry!"

I rushed towards the door, but then remembered that I didn't have a bike. I hurried back into the gymnasium and went to find Adrian. I caught up with him by a stand who'd made some sort of sundial.

"Adrian," I said. "I need to borrow your bike."

He gave me a sceptical look. Adrian doesn't like anyone using his BMX.

"Come on!" I said. "It's an emergency."

Reluctantly he reached into his pocket and gave me his key. "You need to get your bike fixed," he mumbled.

I nodded, ran out of the gymnasium and crossed the schoolyard. I released Adrian's BMX from the bike rack and pedalled as fast as I could. Once I turned off the main road, however, I got off the bike and walked the rest of the way. If I fell on the slippery roads and broke my leg, I definitely wouldn't make it back to school in time.

When I reached my house, I leaned the bike against the wall and unlocked the door. Frank was in his usual spot at the bottom of the stairs, and when I came in he raised his head and paused for a bit, like he couldn't believe I was actually there. Then he hurried towards me and I gave him a quick pat on the head before running upstairs to my room.

I started going through all the papers and mess I had on my desk. I pulled out all the drawers, and rummaged through the contents, but I couldn't find what I was looking for. I ran back downstairs. The photos had to be in the garage.

I opened the garage door, and I had to blink a few times to make sure my eyes were actually seeing what I thought they were seeing. Because in my garage a blue-haired boy was looking back at me. Holding a Mauser M12 hunting rifle.

34

"Mate," I gasped.

"Hey," Niklas said. Maybe he didn't know what else to say because it seemed like a very strange response. Not that I could imagine anything which would be a good response.

"Mate," I repeated. "What are you doing?" My heart was beating so fast in my chest I could hardly hear my own voice.

Niklas looked at the ground. "I wasn't going to shoot him," he whispered.

"What?"

"I swear. I just wanted to scare him."

"Who?"

He looked at the floor. "This whole thing is your fault anyway."

I swallowed. "What happened?"

"Someone from child protection services came to my

house this morning. Of course, everything seemed fine, so they left again. But now I have an even meaner and angrier stepdad. Thanks to you."

"Did he… Did he hurt you?"

Niklas shook his head. "I left the house before he had a chance to." He turned the gun over in his hand. "Right about now my mum will be busy smoothing things over, telling him that we weren't the ones who called them."

"What? Wait, can you please put the gun away? It's making me really nervous to talk to you when you're holding that thing."

"Fine." He shrugged and put the rifle down on the workbench. "It's not like it's loaded or anything. It wasn't like I was actually going to shoot him."

"I know," I said. "Thanks though."

I gestured for us to sit down on a couple of crates by the wall. I figured Sofia was going crazy right about now, trying to call me. My phone was still in my backpack, which I had left at school.

"Why would your mum patch things up with your stepdad? I mean, why doesn't she just leave him?"

He shrugged. "Because in her world the only thing worse than being with a dirtbag is to be alone."

That made no sense to me. "But you can't stay in that house. Not with him."

"I have nowhere else to go."

"What about your dad?"

He shook his head. "I don't talk to him much. He's kind of a deadbeat. Besides, he lives in Oslo."

I rubbed my hands together as I tried to think. I didn't know what to say or how to help him.

"What's up with your hand?"

I looked down at my lap. The asymmetry in my hands and arms is not really too noticeable unless I put them together.

"Oh that." I tried to smile. "Just one of the many perks of having SRS."

He frowned, and it occurred to me that I had never told him. I was so used to people just knowing about it, and apart from my doctor I hadn't actually talked to anyone about it in a really long time.

"Silver-Russell syndrome," I said. "It's a growth disorder."

"You have a growth disorder?" He looked me up and down as if he was checking I was telling the truth.

I nodded.

"Huh, I never knew." He shrugged. "You look like everyone else."

I think that might have been the best thing anyone has ever said to me. Mostly because I really think he actually meant it.

"Yeah, well not exactly." I pointed at myself. "I have a triangular face and my head is too big for my body."

He squinted. "I don't see it."

I looked at him. I'd always felt that my condition was so obvious. The first thing people noticed. "And the arm thing," I said. "My right arm is longer than my left." I held them against each other again to mark my point.

"That's cool though. It kind of makes you look like Barret from *Final Fantasy*."

I laughed. "Growth hormone therapy is what made me taller. But it's stopped working now."

I had no idea why I was telling him all this. I hadn't even said anything to Adrian yet. Maybe it was the fact that he was facing a much bigger problem. In comparison, my problem seemed shallow and sort of silly.

I looked at him. "I might never grow taller than I am right now."

"Really? That sucks."

"Yeah."

"Could be worse though."

"Yeah, could be worse."

"You could be tall and stupid," he grinned.

I laughed. "I guess."

We fell silent. I didn't know what to say, and apparently neither did Niklas as he kept staring at his shoes. After a while he said, "I don't know what to do."

I thought for a minute. "You could stay with us."

"What?"

"I mean, tonight. And for as long as you need. My mum wouldn't mind."

"This isn't the Disney Channel, Sander. I can't live with you."

"You can. For a while, until we figure something else out."

"You think?"

"Definitely. My mum loves you." I got up and put the rifle back in the gun cabinet and locked it. "Let's go to school now, and then after school you'll come home with me."

"I don't know," he replied.

"I'll talk to my mum and explain everything." The thought of Mum taking the handle on this actually created a huge wave of relief. I regretted not telling her sooner. "She'll know what to do."

I got out the stepladder and put the key back in its place.

"Okay."

"Yeah?"

He shrugged. "Yeah, that sounds okay."

We left the garage, and I grabbed Adrian's bike. As we

reached the end of the driveway, Niklas turned left as I turned right.

"Where are you going?"

"I need to stop by my house and get my things."

"What things?"

"You know, my things. My backpack and books. And my PE kit. My teacher will kill me if I forget again."

"But…is it safe?"

"Yeah, it's fine. My stepdad will be at work now."

"Okay…do you want me to come with you?"

"No, that's okay. Don't you have your presentation today?"

"Yeah."

"Well, you should get going. Sofia might actually kill you if you miss it."

"Yeah, okay. I'll talk to you later."

Halfway to school, I realized that I'd forgotten the one thing I went home for in the first place. Sofia would already be furious with me for taking this long. If I returned without the photos I was pretty sure she'd actually murder me.

So I turned around and went back. And when I opened the garage door, the first thing I noticed was that the gun cabinet was wide open. The blue-haired boy wasn't there. And neither was the gun.

35

I reached into my pocket, searching for my phone, before remembering that I didn't have it. It was still back at school. I had to call Mum. Or maybe the police. I had to call someone, but I didn't have a phone and we don't have a landline – so I did the only sensible thing to do in a situation like this.

I went to the town loner, otherwise known as my friend.

Vemund's door was locked. I rang the doorbell over and over, then I yanked the door handle a few times before ringing the doorbell again. Finally the door opened and Vemund appeared in the doorway.

"Sander?" He frowned. "Why are you not in school?"

"I need your help."

"Something tells me that this is not about photography?"

I shook my head and brushed past him into his house.

I gave him a quick summary of the situation, and Vemund went into the next room to call the police.

A few minutes later he came back. "They're going to check it out," he said. "They're on their way."

"Do you have a car? I want to see Niklas."

He shook his head. "I think we'd better let the police handle this."

"I shouldn't have let him go. It's my fault that he's heading over to his stepdad right now, carrying a gun."

Vemund put a hand on my shoulder. "None of this is your fault, Sander. You have done everything you can do for your friend at this point."

I didn't say anything.

"The best thing you can do is to go back to school and let the police handle this. You'll talk to Niklas later. He knows you're there for him."

I left the house, picked up the bike and walked towards school. I knew Vemund was probably right. I couldn't do anything, and the police probably knew what they were doing.

But the police weren't Niklas's friend, and I was.

When I reached the end of the street, I changed my mind and I turned back. I had to stop something bad from happening.

I walked the bike up the long hill leading up to Rosk.

It was slippery in places, but I wouldn't have cycled it anyway, as it was way too steep. I wasn't really sure what my plan was. I just knew that I couldn't go to school without knowing that Niklas was okay.

When I reached the underpass, I got back on my bike and cycled to the other side of the road. I followed the road until I reached the street sign leading down to Roskdalen where Niklas lives. I stopped at the top of his street and paused for a minute. The surface hadn't been salted and it looked very icy.

If I went down the hill I could fall and break an arm or a leg.

I could hit my head on the asphalt and get concussion.

Fabio Casartelli, the famous cyclist, crashed during a Tour de France race. He smashed his head into a rock and died. That was many years ago, but that didn't mean it couldn't happen again. It could happen to me.

I looked down the icy road. Normally I would turn and go around the block. But it would take too much time.

I didn't have time.

So I drew in a breath and took off down the hill.

I turned the bike once I reached a curve. I was going fast. Too fast. I panicked and hit both of the brakes. The wheel started to slide, but the bike didn't stop. Instead it had started going faster and I had no control of it.

I was thrown off the bike and landed on my side.

I sat up. My arm hurt, but apart from that I seemed fine. I picked up the bike and continued cycling. When I reached the end of the street, I could see there was a police car in Niklas's driveway and a large group of people were standing in front of his house.

"What's going on?" one guy said to another.

"No idea," the other replied, shrugging.

I stretched my neck trying to see, but there were too many people in front of me. I asked a tall guy if he could see anything, but he just shook his head. And I realized that I sounded just like them. Suddenly I felt really bad standing there. Niklas would hate it if he saw me here amongst these people. At the same time, I couldn't bring myself to leave.

After a while a police officer came out of the house and asked everyone to move out of the way.

"Back off, please," he said, gesturing with his hands. "Come on, people, back off. There's nothing to see here."

The crowd moved a couple of centimetres, but no one made any effort to actually walk away. I could see the front door of the house opening, but I couldn't really see what was happening. I stepped closer and managed to find a gap between the people in front so I could get a better view.

Then I saw Niklas's stepdad coming out of the house, followed by a policeman.

I kept looking for Niklas, expecting him to come out of the house too, but he never did.

When it comes to the details of what happened that day, it all depends on who you ask.

What the media said (by media, I mean a single tweet by the Police South-West Twitter account): *The police made a house visit in Nærbø around ten o'clock, after a call about a domestic disturbance. A man in his early forties is being questioned by the police.*

What people said:

- Niklas stole a gun and tried to kill his drunken and violent stepdad, but the police showed up and stopped him just in time.

- Niklas and his stepdad fought over the gun, it accidentally went off and Niklas got shot in the arm and is now in the hospital.

- Niklas stole the gun from Sander Dalen's garage. Sander showed up at the scene of the crime and stopped Niklas just in time. (This is also why Sander didn't show up for his presentation the day of the science fair.)

- Niklas shot his stepdad in the leg and is now in juvenile prison.
- Numerous other ridiculous things.

What actually happened: on Monday the 3rd of December, several people driving down Opstad Street called the police and reported they'd seen a boy carrying a weapon. A hunting rifle is not exactly the most discreet thing to carry around in a small town. Or anywhere for that matter. The local police station is a five-minute drive away from Nærbø, but that day there was already a police car in the area dealing with some other issues.

As you might suspect, a boy with a blue Mohawk and a Mauser 12 hunting rifle wasn't too hard to find.

By the time the police received a call saying a young boy was on his way over to Rosklia 36, Nærbø, armed with a rifle, the boy was already sitting in the back of the police car.

On the car ride over to the police station the boy decided he wasn't going to talk. He figured, no matter what happened it would be better to just keep his mouth shut. As long as he didn't say anything there was nothing they could hold him for, or charge him for.

Another car was sent to the address in question while the boy was taken in for questioning. The boy hadn't had breakfast that morning and his stomach was growling. He was given cinnamon buns and fizzy drinks. Everyone at the station was nice to him and made him feel comfortable.

This wasn't why he decided to talk. It was more that he'd reached a point where he had no other options.

The police believed him when he said he wasn't planning on shooting anyone. There were no bullets in the gun. It wasn't even loaded.

He told them everything.

The police talked to the boy's stepdad. He said everything was fine and that the boy was a liar.

The police talked to the boy's mother. She said everything was fine and that the boy was a liar.

The boy took off his shirt and showed them his bruises. Old ones and new ones. He pulled out his phone and showed them a picture recently taken with a pinhole camera at his house.

The boy didn't go back to that house.

He didn't come back to school.

Suddenly everyone knew who I was. I was the guy who kept a gun in my garage. The guy who was at the scene of the crime when the new kid was planning on using that gun on his stepdad.

At school, kids I'd never even talked to would come up to me and say, "Is it true that Niklas shot his stepdad in the leg?" or, "Did you actually prise the gun out of his hands?"

If I didn't answer they would just continue to believe any stupid rumour they'd heard. So normally I would just say, "No, actually, that is not true," and walk away. If I had explained what actually happened it would send out the message that it's okay to talk to people you never bothered talking to before just to get the latest, juicy information. And I didn't want to do that.

While child protection services sorted everything out, Niklas was allowed to take a few days off from school, and he stayed with us for three nights. His case worker had gotten in touch with his dad and it was decided that Niklas should move to Oslo to stay with him.

I Skyped him the day after he left.

"He's still a deadbeat," Niklas said, "but at least he doesn't beat me." And we laughed, even though that wasn't really funny at all.

"Have you talked to your mum?" I asked.

He shook his head. "No. She hasn't made contact, and I'm definitely not going to be the one who gets in touch first. Your mum has called a couple of times though." I smiled. "Yeah, I know."

I couldn't believe that his mum and stepdad were just going about their lives. Like nothing had even happened.

"They're probably finally happy, now that I'm out of their way," Niklas said. He paused for a minute before adding, "I don't want to come back for the trial."

"You have to," I said.

"I know."

"It will be fine."

"Yeah. Look, I have to hang up. Say hi to your mum for me."

I went downstairs to get a drink. My mum was sitting at the kitchen table, drinking coffee.

"Niklas says hi," I said, opening the fridge.

"Oh, how is he?"

I got a glass of orange juice and sat down. "He's good. He's still settling in, I guess."

She took a sip of her coffee and shook her head. "I can't believe his stepdad turned out like that. I mean, I don't really know him, but I do know *his* father and he is such a nice guy. I guess the apple fell pretty far from the tree in his case.

"What does that mean?" I said.

"Just that he is nothing like his dad."

"Neither am I."

She frowned. "Why do you say that?"

I shrugged. "Jakob got his temper. Adrian has his smile. They both have dark hair and broad shoulders."

She tilted her head and looked at me. "In many ways you're the one who is the most like your dad."

"What do you mean?"

"For one, you are kind."

I shrugged. "So is Adrian."

"Of course he is. And so is Jakob."

"If you say so."

She laughed. "Of course all my boys are the nicest, kindest and best little men in the whole world. But you have such a good heart. The way you always put others' needs ahead of your own and make sure everyone else is fine before worrying about yourself. You've done that ever since you were a little boy. Your dad was exactly the same."

"You've never told me that."

She frowned. "I'm sure I have!"

I shook my head.

"Well, I'm telling you now."

38

"Am I late?" Sofia poked her head into my room after a quick knock on the door.

"No, you're just in time," I said. "We were about to call him."

"Great." She walked across the room and sat down on the floor next to Adrian and Filip. "Hey, guys."

"Have you talked to him?" Filip said.

Sofia shook her head and bit her bottom lip. "Not for a few days."

I got my laptop and joined them on the floor. I opened Skype and pressed the video call button next to Niklas's name. After a few seconds the call connected and his face appeared on the screen.

"What's up, losers?" He grinned. He didn't have a blue Mohawk any more. Instead he had a buzz cut.

"Hey, man," Filip said. "How's it going?"

"It's all right. This place is so big. Yesterday, I got lost three times trying to take the subway home."

"Do you know which school you'll go to yet?" Adrian asked.

"Yeah. I start after Christmas. I went for a visit and met the principal and stuff. He seemed all right."

"That's cool."

"He didn't understand me half the time, though. He said southern dialects were really hard to understand."

We laughed, and said stuff like *"Oslo people,"* and *"They are the worst."*

Niklas continued talking about Oslo and how he was getting along better with his dad and how he was adjusting okay to his new life. "That's about it," Niklas said after a while. "How are you guys doing anyway?"

The four of us looked at each other. "You know," I shrugged, "same old."

"Oh, I completely forgot to ask," Niklas said. "How did the science fair go?"

"Well, as this slacker didn't show up –" Sofia said – "I had to save the day." She loved bringing that up. She had given the presentation by herself and then edited the part about the developing process in the report before handing it in.

We didn't get full marks on the project because we

hadn't documented the history of the camera obscura properly or explained in detail what actually happens inside the camera, making it possible to take a picture. So we got a five, but it didn't really matter.

"That's cool," Niklas said. "I knew you'd be okay."

"All right," Sofia said. "We better hang up, we have a party to get to."

"Okay, have fun," Niklas said. He squinted at Sofia. "Well, not *too* much fun."

She laughed. "Call me tomorrow?"

"Yeah."

Erik, one of the guys in my year, was throwing a Christmas party for everyone at school. And, looking around the room, it really seemed like everyone was there. Well, not everyone.

It was funny, because in the beginning I didn't really like having Niklas around, but now I really missed him. By nine thirty everyone was scattered around the room, busy mingling. Filip was standing by a table, showing a magic trick to a group of people who seemed too drunk to pay attention. Sofia was sitting on the couch talking to her friends. Adrian was on the other couch with a girl, talking. Then he had his arm around her. And then they were kissing. Just one of the many things I was sure my little brother would experience before me.

I turned away and looked out the window. It was completely dark outside except for the Christmas lights. I felt a tap on my shoulder and I turned around expecting to see one of my friends. Instead it was a girl in the year below me named Mia. She was holding a wine glass filled with something very red. Too red to be wine.

"Hey," she said. "You're Sander, right?"

I gave her a quick nod and prepared to be asked about Niklas.

"I like your Instagram account."

"You do?"

"Yes, especially the one of the trees in the rain. And the one of the rocks at the beach."

Those posts were super old. She would have had to scroll through my entire account to find them.

"Oh God," she laughed. "I sound like a stalker, don't I?"

I smiled. "No, you're fine."

"You're a really good photographer."

"Thanks."

"You should have more pictures of yourself, though."

"Yeah?"

"Yeah, you're cute." Just then one of her friends came over and put her arm around her.

"Hey, we need you in the kitchen," she told her. "It's time for a group picture."

As they walked away, the girl turned back to me.

"Sorry if Mia here was bothering you. She tends to get pretty chatty after a few sips of cider."

Mia giggled as she let her friend pull her away.

I found a chair, pulled out my phone and started flipping through some old photos. I wanted to post the picture I'd taken at the building site. And I wasn't going to delete it. No matter how few likes it got.

A few days later I put the air back in my tyre and got back on my bike. The streets were still a bit slippery, but it didn't seem too scary any more.

I turned onto Vemund's street and parked my bike outside his house. I didn't bother hiding it in the bushes this time. Vemund had been there for me when I needed him the most. He was a good friend, and I wanted to be a good friend to him too.

For some reason it just didn't seem like the end of the world if someone saw my bike outside his house. I walked up the steps and walked into his house without ringing the doorbell, because in my town that's what good friends do.

Vemund was sitting in his chair, listening to classical music.

"Sander!" he said. "What can I do for you today?"

"I'm just visiting," I said. "How are you?"

"I'm fine, thank you." He smiled. "And yourself?"

"I'm good."

"Good. You know I still have the negatives from the Olympus film, if you'd like to continue the process?"

We went down to the basement, and Vemund showed me how to make the negatives photo-sized using the photo enlarger and then we developed them as normal.

I put a negative in the first tray and used the tongs to flip it a few times. I shook the tray a bit, as it felt like doing something active would make it develop faster.

"How's Niklas doing?" Vemund said.

"He's fine. I think he's still settling in, but he's good."

"Very good. I'm glad to hear that."

Once the picture was ready I moved it to the next tray and Vemund took over.

He turned and looked at me. The safelight made his face red and shiny. "What's this?"

"Oh." It was the picture I had taken of the angel and the broken glass. "I took it on your driveway. I sort of liked the idea of having something nice among everything that's broken."

He smiled. "This is a very good picture. You really have an eye for detail."

"Thanks. You can keep it if you want."

"Are you sure?"

I nodded. "Can I ask you a question?"

"Ask away."

"What did you think about me when you first met me?"

"What do you mean?"

"In the church. When we met for the first time. What did you think about me?"

He shrugged. "I thought you were a boy who was interested in photography."

"But did you think I looked normal?"

"Define normal."

I guess Vemund wasn't really the right person to ask about this.

He moved the photo to the last tray. "You know, there was one thing I always used to say to the kids I was working with."

"What?"

"Try not to worry so much about what other people think of you. All you can do is be you."

He made it sound so simple. "You think that works?"

Vemund smiled. "It worked for me."

The 18th of December – it was time for my check-up.

When I was younger I was always a bit nervous about going to the hospital, so Mum decided we should play different car games on our way over to keep my mind occupied. And since then it had sort of become a tradition. One of our games is called Fake News. We take turns coming up with statements and the other has to guess whether it's true or not. You're allowed one follow-up before deciding, but then you'll only get half a point.

As we exited the highway, Mum said, "Did you hear about the guy who starved to death trying to beat the world record in fasting?"

"Nope. That didn't happen."

"Are you sure?"

"Positive."

"Okay, you're right. Your turn."

"Did you hear about the man who won the lottery, with help from his chicken?"

She thought for a minute. "Okay, go on."

"He dropped some corns on his calculator and the chicken picked them off and ended up clicking numbers on it. The man played the numbers in the lottery and won."

She shook her head. "Fake news."

"Wrong. It happened."

"No way!"

"Hundred per cent."

Mum pulled into the hospital car park. "Are you nervous?" she asked.

I shook my head and looked out the window. There was nothing to be nervous about, because I already knew what the results would be. The treatment wasn't working any more.

Mum turned off the engine and unbuckled her seat belt. "Ready?"

"Ready."

I knew this would be the time my doctor would take me off the treatment and tell me I most likely wouldn't grow any more. But somehow, I felt strangely okay crossing the car park. No matter what happened, I would still be me. Sander Dalen. One in a Hundred Thousand.

ONE in A HUNDRED THOUSAND

DISCUSSION QUESTIONS

CONTAINS SPOILERS

- Had you heard of Silver-Russell Syndrome before reading *One in a Hundred Thousand*? How does it affect Sander's life? Is he treated differently by people because of it?

- Compare and contrast what we hear about Old Kaland, and what we know about Vemund. How did you feel when you discovered they were the same person?

- Some of the things Vemund chooses to do seem eccentric to his neighbours. Why do you think he does these things, irrespective of what other people think?

- Think about Sander and his brothers, and other sibling groups you know in real life. How do you think birth order influences individual personalities and family dynamics? How do you think Sander's SRS plays into this?

- Look at pages 138-140. What do you think about the way in which Niklas talks about his relationship with Sofia? Why do you think it provokes Sander? What other things does Niklas do that irritate Sander?

- Sander loves photography, but doesn't seem to like Instagram and is resistant to include it in his school project. Why do you think this is? How has Instagram changed the way people take photos? Is this for the better or worse?

- What do you think Sander and Sofia's different attitudes towards their shared science project say about their personalities? Which one are you most like?

- Sander is the least keen on Niklas at the start of the novel, but ultimately is the one who picks up on the problems he's having at home. Why do you think he notices things that others might not? Can you go back through the novel and identify any clues that indicate that Niklas is having problems at home?

- Think about the title of the novel. How does Sander feel about being one in a hundred thousand? Has this changed by the end?

ABOUT THE AUTHOR

Linni Ingemundsen works as a freelance writer, translator and cartoonist and has changed jobs and addresses more times than she can count.

She has worked as a dishwasher in Australia, a voluntary journalist in Tanzania, and has approximately 2.5 near-death experiences behind her. Still, what truly inspires her writing is her background growing up in a village on the south-western coast of Norway.

Some of her favourite things in life include chocolate, cats and her yellow typewriter.

Linni's debut novel, *The Unpredictability of Being Human* was nominated for the CILIP Carnegie medal in 2019.

Turn the page to read an extract.

If I got to be God for one day, the first thing I'd do would be to microwave a bag of popcorn to perfection. Where all the corns got popped and not a single corn burned. And then I'd make sure that everyone else who made popcorn that day had their bags cooked to perfection too. I think a lot of people would be happy that day.

The next thing I might do is to take back what happened that day in Holberg's shop, because that was pretty silly. But then again, maybe I wouldn't undo it, because if I hadn't shoplifted that day I wouldn't have met Hanna Kjerag. You might ask why I don't change things around so that I met Hanna anyway, but I don't think it works that way. I think that's cheating.

I'd like to say that I'd end world hunger and create world peace and fix everything else that's wrong in this world. But I honestly wouldn't touch any of that. I figure that if it was *that* easy, God would have taken care of it all a long time ago. Who knows what sort of trouble I'd stir up if I started messing with that on my first day on the job?

So I'd stick to simpler things, like popcorn. Popcorn can't cause too much trouble. Besides, it's the small things in life that matter. That's what my Norwegian teacher, Trude Fjell, says.

My name is Malin Sande and I am fourteen years old. Last week I was given a school assignment: What would you do if you got to be God for one day?

I failed.

I failed because they said I didn't take the task seriously. All the kids who said that they wanted to get rid of world hunger passed.

I live in Haasund together with just about 5,346 other people. Unless you're from Haasund or any of the neighbouring villages, you won't have heard about the place.

Haasund is a village on the south-western coast of Norway. To get to my house you go up Haugen Hill, which is right next to Hopstad Butcher's. Then you just continue straight ahead until you reach Thorstein Street. At the end of the street there is a great big red house. It has a huge yard, with grass cut to perfection and a privet hedge surrounding it. On each side of the driveway, two tall birch trees have formed an arch almost welcoming you in. It really is a magnificent house.

I live in the house next to it. The white one with the broken garage door. It should have been painted last summer and the lawn hasn't been mowed in a while. You'll see it when you see it.

Malin knows she can't fix the big stuff in her life. Instead she watches from the sidelines, as her dad yells, her brother lies and her mum falls apart. At least after she meets Hanna she has a friend to help her. Because being Malin is complicated – learning how to kiss, what to wear to prom, and what to do when you upset the prettiest, meanest girl in school.

It's tough fitting in when you're different.
But what if it's the world that's weird, not you?

A beautiful, funny and honest coming-of-age story that never pretends life is perfect.

Nominated for CILIP Carnegie Medal 2019

"Coming-of-age narratives about dysfunctional families and mean girls at school are common, but this is exceptional." *The Sunday Times*

"Features a beguiling heroine at that most tricky stage of metamorphosis, from child to adult…full of humour and pathos." *The Financial Times*

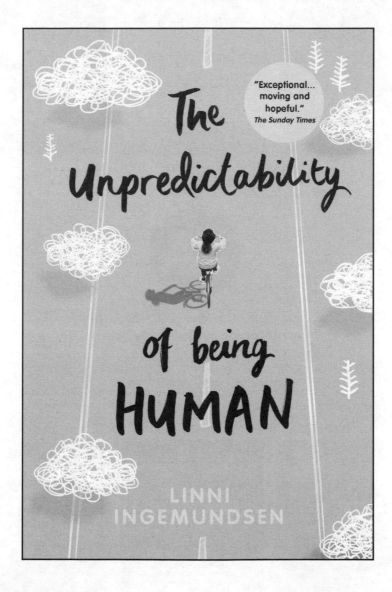

The
Unpredictability

of being

HUMAN

LINNI
INGEMUNDSEN

Love this book? Love Usborne YA

Follow us online and sign up to the Usborne YA
newsletter for the latest YA books,
news and competitions:

usborne.com/yanewsletter

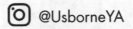 @UsborneYA

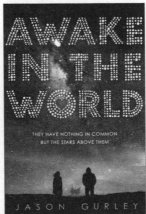

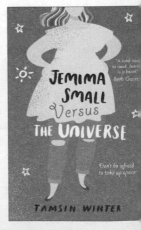